just for comfort

just for comfort

ralph osborne

a misFit
book

INSOMNIAC PRESS

Edited by Michael Holmes.
Designed by Mike O'Connor.

Canadian Cataloguing in Publication Data

Osborne, Ralph, 1943-
   Just for comfort

ISBN 1-895837-63-4

1. Title.

PS8579.S355J87 2000   C813'.6   C00-930477-0
PR9199.3.O82J87 2000

The publisher gratefully acknowledges the support of the Canada Council, the Ontario Arts Council and Department of Canadian Heritage through the Book Publishing Industry Development Program.

Printed and bound in Canada

Insomniac Press, 192 Spadina Avenue, Suite 403, Toronto, Ontario, Canada, M5T 2C2
www.insomniacpress.com

ACKNOWLEDGEMENTS

Michael Holmes, my editor, is an exceptional and brilliant man. This book might never have seen the light of day without his sure, insightful and capable mentoring. I count myself extremely fortunate to have run into him. I owe him a tremendous debt of gratitude.

I also owe Clint Bomphray and Michael Hubar, whose lifelong dedication to their art has always inspired me. And thanks to (Dr.) Ross Gray, who helped get the ball rolling.

Thanks, as well, for their invaluable help to: Ariane Blackman, Hazel Goldman, Mary Kane, Maia Kareda, Lillian Lahe, Junji Nishihata, Rhona Singer, Karen Whalen, Sue Cantan, Duff Kaufman and Laura Marks.

Last, but by no means least, thank you, Michael O'Connor.

In Memorium

John Rafter and Ted Poole; two guys who would have
loved to have been around to see this published.

For Tam, the truest beauty, and my partner in all things.

chapter one

The logistics of disposing of a dead body were perplexing me when the doorbell rang. I mean, we see it all the time on TV and in the movies: you nudge them over a cliff or roll them in a carpet, drag them to the dumpster and, bam, you're there. Of course slicing or sawing is out of the question — I'm extremely squeamish when it comes to other people's blood. Mind you, it's a nausea provoked mostly by movies and television — since that's where I've experienced the bulk of gore. Actually, I haven't experienced it, just seen the pictures. And the odd thing is that when confronted with actual bloody scenes in real life, things I can't avoid having to deal with and can't pass off, I'm the next best thing to a doctor or an emergency medic. You want me to be the cut man in your corner.

When I was six I saw an older kid of nine or ten lying on the tailgate of a half-ton, waiting for an ambulance. From his matted hair to one shoeless foot he was covered in blood — it seeped from a thousand cuts. Something to do with a road grader; probably gravel surfing. I never forgot the image of the shivering boy bathed in crimson, surrounded by big people with furrowed brows chanting the plainsong of "There, there, you'll be okay," while waiting with some urgency for someone to take charge and make it okay for them as well.

I was staring, wide-eyed, taking it all in in the approaching twilight and appreciating it for what it was — yet another truly amazing sight — when, goddammit, I was spotted by one of the big people, one of the big, stupid people, and roughly propelled on a vector that would see me home safe and at my customary time of "Where have you been, do you know how late it is?"

Anyway, I could always handle the monotony of blood and bruises when I had the restaurant. Every electric slicer cut, knife wound, scald, fat burn, missing fingertip and dislocation ended up at my door and I dealt with it all. First you have to get them to pry their hands away from the injury to get a good enough look to make the diagnosis, and then keep it — and them — together until you can make the handoff to somebody that actually knows what the fuck they're doing.

But at the movies, where I have a choice, I'm down on the floor searching for the popcorn if there's even a hint of impending gore. The bottom line is if you show me your cut I'll help you, but if you show me a picture of your cut I'll find a way to get even when I come to.

So cutting, sawing or slicing the corpse with the concomitant sighs, farts and gurgles would be a method born of such desperation for me that it would be almost better not to do the job at all.

Bing, bong. Again that ridiculous bell. Right out of an Avon commercial. It was not at all conducive to resolving my disposal issue. I had been experimenting with the carpet method and standing there with a hundred and ten pounds wrapped in what could only be seen as a huge velvet monstrosity of a portrait of a matador in the classic Veronica pose. Only my pal Weilander would have the kind of taste needed to acquire this poetically perfect shroud, whose prior duty was to cover his even more pathetic couch. But it was haiku I was now hearing, after the fashion of Basho:

> late night deepening
> the sound of a ringing bell
> making goosebumps rise

This is an omen. I hate bells. And their drooling, simpering cousins, the chimes. They occupy the netherworld between music and noise. One tiny note at the end of a symphonic movement may well be the bell's finest moment. It's a slippery, clanging, cacophonous downhill slide after that. School bells, church bells, fire alarms, and your well-meaning-but-idiotic neighbour's wind chimes can exact quite a toll. Alarm clocks and telephones clinch the argument: the nature of a bell is essentially hostile.

It's obviously somebody for Weilander. Since I just accepted his hospitality on a whim, when I ran into him at the airport, nobody would even know I was here. That was what, a few hours ago? Of the few people who might have expected me at this time of year, no one would know exactly when I would arrive. Weilander, who was air freighting a specimen to the coast when I ran into him, was gone for the weekend. "Two or three days, eh," he said, then we would catch up on old times.

A-von. I'm going to have to deal with this since Quasimodo is not, apparently, about to leave. Hmm, what to do? A quick tug on the velvet shroud tells me that moving my burden even the few feet that would put it behind the couch will require too much effort. Fuck, I'm still sweating from rolling her up. Any more exertion and my face will turn that shade of boiled pink that proclaims: "Guilty, Your Honour, as anyone can see!" Usually, at this time of year, the evenings are quite nippy. Who would have thought that it would be so warm or that you'd practically need a forklift to carry this slender little thing?

To get to the door, I hop and skip in a jerky squirrel-like motion. Damn. No peephole. Looking back, at least, I can't see the bundle. Neither can anyone, I figure, from the door. This will be a good lesson, if I survive. In my best how-dare-you-disturb-me fashion I yank the door open: ready for fight, not flight.

There stands Ray, the giant forest gnome, the hairy beast. A greasy, malodorous, scruffy, egg-sucking hound who walks like a man. Ray, the antithesis of order, enterprise and clean laundry. Dear and gentle Ray, the anticlimax. Ray, the slightly portly, demented pirate who talks like a girl. Old friend Ray.

"Jesus, Ray, it's almost midnight," I say, somewhat relieved.

"I saw the light," he says, his voice a shocking falsetto trill in a basso profundo body.

"Great, Ray. Great. Perhaps you'll share that with me one day but ..."

"No. Your light." Sad-eyed Ray, now smiling almost. Giaconda Ray.

"Did you bring any drugs at least?" I joke, since the idea of Ray being able to supply even so much as a roach would amuse anyone who knew him. He was a master at living simply.

"Well," he said softly, "I thought you might have some." Those eyes. Like a bloodhound, just finished a good howl at the moon and waiting for the results to come in.

"G'night, Ray." Slowly I started to close the door. Ray was grinning.

"You're up to somethinggg," he trilled in the singsong way that kids have when they tease.

"Yes, Ray, I am." I paused. "Perhaps you had better come in."

Whenever he enters any civilized place, Ray becomes, for a moment, oddly formal. Oliver Hardy meets the Duchess. He steps oh so lightly, tiptoe almost, through the door and stops. With his hands clasped primly together he tilts his head slightly, purses his lips and rolls his eyes up, and around, and down, looking everywhere but at his host. Like a stray in the kitchen he is entranced by the wonder of it all, the promise of new delights, all the while trembling and poised to flee.

"Come in, Ray. Come in."

"Thank you." He said, and, in the prairie custom of removing your footwear so as not to track in the gumbo, he stooped towards his feet.

"No, Ray," I said quickly. "Leave your boots on. It's okay." More than okay, really. Necessary, in fact.

"Thank you," he said again, most proper. Butter wouldn't melt in his mouth. Looks as if it had in his beard.

"Au contraire. Thank you." The Alphonse-Gaston routine aside, I wasn't kidding. One time I saw Ray with his shoes off; a big toe ripped through his grimy sock, a ridged, curly nail jutting out a half inch, looking like a used trowel caught in a tornado. See something like that and it even takes a while to notice the smell. Part of the strategy I suspect.

"Before we go any further, Ray, I have to tell you that I am up to something. My advice to you is to leave. Now." I watched him take this in. Raindrops on an elephant's hide.

"Well," he said, almost shyly. "I am a trifle peckish."

"You're hungry, Ray, is that it?" With Ray that was always it. The black hole known as Ray's appetite. The trans-fatty acid hunger that never sleeps.

Ray, saying nothing, rapidly nodded his head up and down. Yes. Yes. Yes. Doggie want a bone. Alert. Eyes at attention.

"Okay, Ray, but this is big and you're going to have to keep your mouth shut." A look of mock concern on Ray's face. "Except when you're eating, of course." Now mock relief. "Forever, Ray. Or I'll have to kill you."

Ray, with merry eyes, pulls an imaginary zipper across his mouth, mimes locking it and throwing away the key. You can tell him anything. He'll listen like your favourite retriever, lying there, almost dreaming, with only the sporadic and half-hearted thump of his tail to show he's listening. Ray is the Buddha who gets fat on the mysteries you dish up. He loves secrets. He keeps secrets. Ray eats secrets like candy bars.

Damn, it was great to see him. I was beginning to feel better. Back in charge. I found Ray. I helped Ray once. Now he will help me forever. And although a few flagons and the odd haunch tossed his way was most gratefully received it was never, ever necessary. I was so relieved I fucking near gave him a hug, recovering my senses just in time. Nevertheless the gesture was noted by Ray and duly appreciated.

I turn out the living room light as we walk through to the kitchen, watching Ray closely. He sees the large cocoon on the floor and loses his dreamy look — slap, slap, slap — like an old-fashioned window blind coiling around itself. He focuses, eyes narrower, then lets it go and keeps moving. (Good, Ray. Very good.) In the kitchen during the first few seconds, I stare at Ray, his eyes everywhere but on me. Then coyly, playfully, they zero in on the fridge. He strains forward just a bit, on point. What's done is done. Whatever it is, the past is past. All is forgiven. Feed me.

"It'll have to be cold pizza, Ray. Weilander doesn't have a microwave."

"Yummm," says Ray, as if it were pheasant.

I pulled the upright handle on the old Westinghouse, the "chrome boner" as Weilander calls it, ever the visceral guy. The ancient tractor motor powering the fridge abruptly cut out and in the emphatic quiet came a sudden appreciation of the dilemma in which I had placed myself. I was almost trapped. In my mind I heard those sucking sounds, the little whimpers, the moans and slurps. Ray, the one-man band of injudicious noises, was about to eat.

The first time I ever saw Ray was at Myta's Café: a small-city-chic, cordon-Bleu-trained-little-rich-girl-owned, beige and chrome neutral toned, lots of flowers and a few pieces of very good art, kinda place. It was close to the courthouse and the fringe of the A-list office towers named after banks. Daddy Bean, big-time lawyer, was the financial backer. All done legally, of course, at prime plus one with suitable penalties for non-performance. Mummy Bean, by dint of being married to Daddy Bean, was one of the head ladies on various museum and gallery boards. Neither of them ever missed lunch, with Daddy permanently affixed to the bar (ever the lawyer) and Mummy alternately harrassing the wait staff — who were themselves all siblings and cousins of Myta's or friends from very good families — and manning the till. The clientele were the usual mix of local who's whos, professionals and power dressers. Important people from out of town were squired there for lunch by hosts who didn't need to take out a small bank loan to pay for it.

One Friday lunch, late-ish, I endured a short wait listening to the deputy minister of health talking golf to a judge. Behind me the lineup for the second rush was filling up with art students and librarians. It was just before I opened my own restaurant and I was hoping to talk to Myta about kitchen staff. Victoria — Mummy Bean — seemed a trifle more agitated than usual until she spotted me. She left off whipping the busboy, who escaped to the kitchen, and visibly brightened. Oh oh. Danger. Danger. She turned to one of her daughters — Vanilla, I think, the tall, blonde, leggy one in a family of diminutive brunettes — and whispered something while looking straight at me. Myta was a friend. Victoria not.

I was shown to the end of a row of deuces along a mirrored banquette in the overflow section opposite the bar. There, in a semi-circle of oily calm, sat Ray. A petunia in the corner, ignored by all the onions. If he had been lying on the sidewalk they could have stepped around him and kept going. But no. Ray, the bloated carcass washed up on the shore of their exclusivity, was making them all less special. Outside the circle, waiters were bustling, brightly bejewelled lady realtors were waving their cellphones, and everywhere threesomes of the perfectly coiffed were jammed into tables for two. Inside the arc of which Ray was the hub, and just beside him, was an empty table. My table. The last seat in the house at The Twilight Zone Café.

I sat on the banquette a scant thirty inches from this apparition. As I was surreptitiously giving him the once-over I caught a whiff of what must have been high-powered cologne mixed with insecticide. It had a very definite bass note of day-old manure, ripe but not insistent. Jesus! On the plus side, I noted faint areas of residue on his shirt where you could see that he had gone to a lot of trouble scraping off old bits of food, birdshit, and whatever, to make himself presentable. Any sign of grooming is healthy.

In contrast to Ray's appearance, the plate in front of him — and the knife and fork casually arranged on top — were spotless. Scattered around the plate was a confetti of dark crumbs. Ray was alternately licking his index fingertip and stabbing flecks of bread that he would bring to his lips and spear with his tongue. Froggy Ray. Covert stares and indignant snorts of disbelief were popping off all around him like flashbulbs at a wedding. Ray was too intent on rounding up all the little dogies to notice.

His table was banked up beside a partition that led to the kitchen. From behind it a head appeared; a long, skinny, pasty-faced head with giant eyelashes, a wispy mustache and a curly pink mini-afro. "Pssst, Ray," he tinkled. "She says she already has somebody for the job. Sorree." A hand appeared below the head and put a twenty on Ray's table.

"Thank you," said Ray, taking the money as the head disappeared. His mouth set a little as he looked down at his gleaming plate.

Vanilla arrived to clear Ray's table and delicately presented him with the bill. Ray picked it up between thumb and forefinger with the added flourish of an extended pinkie and looked at the total. Stylish, I thought, even in defeat.

"How much is the cheesecake?" he asked.

Vanilla, who had obviously seen the handoff from the

kitchen, replied a little sadly, "Six ninety-five," in a tone that distinctly said, "You can't afford it, buddy."

At that point — and I'm seemingly powerless to stop these urges — I leaned towards Ray's feet on a variant of the old quarter-behind-the-ear trick. Gasp. Close call. Sandbagged by a stronger, nearer, eau-de-dung odour, I almost lost it, pulling out of the tailspin just in time. "Excuse me," I say to Ray, "but I couldn't help but notice this drop from your pocket," as I hand him another twenty.

Ray, confused, quizzical eyes, looks at me, then the money. And he gets it. "Why, thank you," he smiles shyly. Turning to Vanilla he says, "I'll have the chocolate Grand Marnier, please." His pronunciation startlingly perfect. "With extra whipped cream."

"And I'll have some of that puréed swill you call soup," I say jokingly, if a bit too loud. She took both orders and gave Ray and me a very sweet smile. Hmm. I'm going to have to have a closer look at that girl. Everyone, it seems, enjoys thwarting Mummy.

Ray, elbows on the table, palms flat together in front of his nose, thumbs hooked under his chin, praying maybe, says, looking straight ahead, "That was not necessary, but very kind. Thank you."

I say, "S'okay. I'm sure you would have done the same for me." Ray, on one of the very few occasions since I've known him, turned and looked me right in the eye. There was some steel back there, I noted. "Yes," he said, "I would."

The cheesecake snaps him out of it. He forgets me, the room he's in, everything. His eyes are brimming with ardour. A pinky red tongue tip pops out on one side of his mouth, slides across his upper lip and gets sucked back out of sight like a drooling cartoon wolf. There is a muted humming noise. Ray, the Tasmanian devil. Half-joining in the fun, and half in self-defence, I start slurping my soup in a way that would please a Shanghai hostess. Victoria was not amused.

Ray's humming got louder, interrupted in bursts by

juicy smacks. He leisurely ran his tongue up one side of the fork and down the other, and followed this with a long, slow sound that a wet vacuum might make, accompanied by a low-throated growl. Peripherally I could see a rash of people looking at their watches. "Would you look at the time!" As for Porno Ray, licking and diving and darting at his dessert over and over again, I was thinking that if cheesecake were a large-breasted woman it would actually have been a more palatable scene. One minute and fifty-five seconds after the dessert arrived, the tail end of stampeding diners cleared the room just as Ray was dabbing the last of the whipped cream from the corner of his mouth. It sounded like liposuction, but it wasn't as pretty to watch. Forget about slabs of rotting meat or paintings of body parts, Ray had just taken performance art to a new level.

"Enjoy that, did you?" I asked.

"Mmmm." Ray rolls his eyes and pats his tummy. And then, a trifle greedily, "You're not eating your soup. Were you planning on finishing?"

As it turned out Ray was on his way to court and needed a job. I had found my dishwasher slash kitchen guy. There were downsides. I would be forced on too many occasions — more than one, say — to see Ray eat. And I could never stand in a room with my back to Victoria. But when our restaurant war heated up I would send Ray over to Myta's and treat him to a Friday lunch.

"Tell you what, Ray," I say, tossing him the pizza box, "finish this off. Help yourself to a beer if there is one. There's something I have to do in the other room."

"No beer, thank you, this is just fine," he trills.

"Whatever, Ray." And I escape to the crypt-like silence of the living room.

Poole might have called it a parlour — given its funereal content. I ask myself what he would have done, since his opinion was one of the very few I ever cared about. He was my friend, mentor, acid guru and, despite a thirty-year age difference, a true kindred spirit. He died a few months ago. If he could have held on for another year, he might have outlasted me. I don't want to think about that. Death held no terror for Poole. As far as he was concerned, he was merely stepping through the portal — and into the next adventure. He would not have approved of this business, nor would he have censured my actions.

Some good advice? Whenever you don't know what to do, don't do anything. Perhaps a truer take is: whenever you don't know what to do, step off the stage. Poole used to say this — one of many things we would aver before embarking on psychedelic journeys. We would have some form of ceremony, and it would be part of the litany. Don't do anything. Step off the stage. Don't be hard on yourself. Brothers, let us agree to forgive one another. Forgive one. Forgive all. Yes, all true.

Forgive even this stupid, greedy little bitch, done in by her own desires? A chip shot into an open net with a magnificent assist from me?

Yes, I must forgive even her.

Timing a bit off on that one. Oh well.

I can't blame Ray for my indecision. His visit has made me a little giddy. I work best solo. Still, in an odd way, it's a comfort having him here. The skirmish in the kitchen is all but won, and quiet once again intrudes. All that remains is for Ray to do a few victory laps. Water from a bowl, crumbs from the box. Those kind of laps. A throat clears ever so slightly. There is a barely audible knock on the door frame. Ahem. Tap tap.

"Finished so soon, Ray?"

"I was famished," he says, appearing to be surprised at such an anomaly.

I am on the couch, at least that's what it must have been at one time. Weilander has the same relationship to furniture as Ray does to clothing. Well, almost. In part it's his environmentalism: why cut down a perfectly good cushion or tear up some virgin fabric when there's a lot of sitting left in this baby? Ray takes the threadbare chair with the two different seat cushions piled on top of one another.

Between us there's some kind of hand-built coffee table, nailed together, with a top of two weathered barn boards someone's given up trying to carve on. In addition to being a top-notch environmental expert and ornithologist of some repute, Weilander was a skilled taxidermist. On the far wall, mounted on a plaque, a huge pheasant looked like it was about to take off. Below that, on a low table, a raccoon eyeballed some waxed eggs. Just past the far side of the couch, and only partially visible, a large stuffed velvet pita lay sullenly on the floor.

"You should probably catch that before it dries," I say, pointing to a tomatoey bit coagulating on Ray's beard. Ray plucks it off, examines it and tosses it down the hatch. Attempting a lightheartedness I did not feel I said, "That's a poor man's dessert, Ray."

"You said that was the stuff you picked from your teeth." Pedantic Ray.

"It's both, Ray. Apples and bananas. Both fruit. Ray?"

"Yass?"

"I know this is going to be a slightly touchy subject for you — but do you think it's wrong, under any circumstance, to deliberately kill one's daughter-in-law?"

He gave it a moment and then, "Yass. Probably it is. Legally, for sure."

Can you kill your daughter-in-law? Of course not. Which is why I had to hurry and get the job done before the wedding. Before my little boy pranced in public in a red — pardon, burgundy — suit derived from a dimwitted ten-year-old's bridal fantasy. She would of course look good as Barbie in white.

My job was to get Ken to switch to black for the funeral; then burn the clothes as a purification rite and move on.

Still, I have Ray to deal with. Why is he here anyway?

Good thought. Why indeed? Everything had been going according to plan until Ray appeared. Well, the action part at least — there really wasn't a plan so much as a spontaneous embracing of circumstance. I have to admit, the needle was stuck in the "Now what?" groove when Ray rang the bell. That's the problem with these hastily contrived schemes. All one sees is the action part. But action begets consequence.

It works well in sports. In fact it is the essence of sports. Hang a curveball up and over and chances are it'll cost you. Ditto, if you settle for the double axel instead of the triple toe loop. It's all done within a ruled structure and a managed time frame. Fuck up and there's another game, another competition. This is different: no structure to speak of and no time frame except the sooner, the better. With murder, overtime begins after the sudden death.

"Things that are illegal aren't necessarily wrong, are they, Ray?" We both had a chuckle over that.

"No," he says, visibly relieved.

"And things that are wrong aren't necessarily illegal, are they?"

"You are correct, sir. Ha. Ha. Ha." Ray says in his best Ed-to-Johnny imitation. I forgot how much fun I used to have with this guy.

"Well, Raymundo, I've had quite an evening. I'd like to share it with you but if I do it will put you in an awkward position."

"I wish." Says Ray, a little wistfully.

"What do you mean?" I said, glaring at him.

"Mmm? Nothing. Just kidding," he said quickly.

"Anyway, Ray," I look pointedly to the body wrapped in the godawful rug, "if you leave now you're not involved. Stay and you are. Last chance, old friend, there are moves to be made."

"I'm not going anywhere. This is too interesting."

"Yes. It's interesting all right. And by the way, what brought you here tonight? How did you know I'd be here?

Or are you suddenly great pals with Weilander?"

"Goodness, no. But I did run into him and he said you'd be here."

"What?"

"He said you'd be here. He gave me the address, although I don't think he wanted to. He said he'd just missed you at the bar, that he needed to get a bite at Georgie's, but he'll be home later."

"Oh fuck. That asshole! Jesus, he's not supposed to be back for two days. That fucking Weilander. He never could follow a script. Joe loosey goosey. Don't sweat it, man, the universe will unfold as it should. Asshole!"

Ray bit his bottom lip and hunched his shoulders. Waiting.

"For fucksakes, Ray, you should have said something."

"Well I was just about to." A little defensively. "I mean, I just did."

"Never mind. Just give me a hand with this. Quick!" I said, and grabbed the end of the rug-wrapped corpse.

chapter two

You wouldn't think it to look at her, but I could believe she was so heavy by the way she occupied space. My space.

When Donald called and said he was bringing her to meet me, I was happy for him. She looked good on paper. It was a few months after we had reconciled from his latest bout of what could charitably be described as selective Tourette's syndrome. The phone would ring. I'd answer, "Hello." On the other end a stream of curses would begin. It started with, "Yeah, ya fuck ya," and continued unabated until I'd hang up. He was drunk, of course, and in need of something, as ever. Usually, but not always, money. And such a foul-mouthed little fucker. Just, as with most things, like his mummy dearest. I could never see much of myself in him. Regardless of this and the fact I'd been propelled out of his life when he was three, I tried.

One morning I opened the door to a still handsome Donald, despite the stubble and bleary eyes. Up all night to make the early flight. We hugged.

"This," he said, "is Ananah."

She stopped chewing her gum and said hello, offering a quick, dry hand and briefly enduring an embrace. Donald was beaming through the blear.

She was not skinny, but very slender. Pretty enough, with thin blonde shoulder-length hair and straight-cut bangs that stopped just above her eyebrows. Her leggings and tank top were skin-tight, making her look younger than she really was. But Ananah's eyes got me. Perhaps it was the dilated pupils. I would speak to her and she'd look — where? Over my shoulder? Into space? Her extremely long eyelashes would point off into the distance and blink like some kind of ship-to-ship code while she waited for you to stop. That's when I realized that in looks, as well as demeanour, she bore a striking resemblance to a goat in a petting zoo.

Every twenty minutes or so Ananah would jump up and head for the bathroom. "Man, she's great, isn't she? She's so great," Donald would say, swigging on a breakfast beer. After a while she didn't even take enough care to wipe away the little smudges of white powder around her reddening nostrils. I didn't ask Donald about his limp or the cast covering his right hand. No doubt he would tell me all about it after a few more rounds.

Dead, she weighed considerably more than a goat, I thought, as Ray and I struggled to get her through the kitchen and out the back door. Part of the problem was trying to make sure that no piece of the rug touched me except where I gripped the folds. A heavy, pendulous, sagging bundle of uneviscerated meat, she was creeping me out more than just a little. Carrying a dead rat by the tail — times twenty. And because I was trying to hold the body away from me I could feel my back start to pop.

"Ray, hold it a sec. I have to put her down to open the door."

"Okaay," he said calmly, as if I were asking him to hold my coat.

I fumbled and stalled a bit to rest. It was occurring to me that I hadn't planned this at all well. Ray, no doubt sensing my need to stretch the moment, asked, "How long since you ah, um, how long has she been wrapped in this rug?" He was still holding her feet aloft.

"Fuck, Ray, I don't know. A few hours. Why?" I snapped.

"Just asking." And then: "Where were you going to take her?"

The sudden irritation I felt was again due to my lack of planning. Not Ray's fault. I swallowed the bile. It was time for me to bite it and start thinking with the clarity and precision for which I am all too seldom noted. For example, I hadn't even intended to kill her. It was just a whim. I lucked into a certain set of circumstances and took advantage. The downside being that I hadn't quite worked everything out.

Weilander's old bungalow is on a dead-end street, a few houses away from a bicycle path that snakes around the edge of town. There is a creek beside the path. It doesn't really go anywhere. Running from the man-made lake in the middle of the city to a few miles outside of town, it dwindles down to a trickle and disappears into a marshy slough. Dogs, bicycles, kids, people with strollers, are forever wandering by. There's even a bit of canoe practice that goes on, although you can only ever paddle a half mile or so before you have to portage across a busy street. Also, the local diving club would periodically embark on a creek cleanup, retrieving rusted shopping carts, bicycle parts, lamps, and old tires from the filthy ooze. The upside, however, is that it's visibly impenetrable through the mud and murk. And, given the proper weights, it is plenty deep enough to swallow Ananah.

"I don't know, Ray." I tried to answer his question. "Maybe dump her in the creek. I was trying to work all this out when you showed up." My tone suggested perhaps he was part of the problem.

"Oh?" says Ray, eyebrows arched, not buying into it at all. "It's just that I was wondering how you did it. How you, you know, killed her?"

"Now? You want to know that right now?"

"Well," says Ray, looking pointedly at the feet he was still holding. "I am kind of up in the air about it." He snorted, biting his lip.

I exploded into laughter.

It wasn't right. It was ... something ... I don't know, disrespectful. Certainly not very Zen. Hysteria, perhaps. The more I tried to compose myself, the more I laughed.

Ray shook so hard that his end of the rug flipped open and a black platform sandal dropped out. There was a brief pause and then we roared even louder.

Then the doorbell rang. It was followed by three loud knocks, then five more in rapid succession.

Ray took the lead. The part of me that was not terror-stricken admired the hell out of him for that.

"You get the door and I'll take her down here," he said, motioning to the basement stairs.

Brave Ray picked up the bundle, threw it easily over his shoulder, and gingerly picked his way down into the blackness. As I turned to answer the front door I saw the shoe. I kicked it quickly into the void.

"Ouch," came a silly little subterranean voice.

"You're an asshole, Ray. You know that?"

By the time I open the door and see who's making all the racket, I'm very calm.

"Yes, officer, what can I do for you at this late hour?"

I'm looking at a cop. A six-two, large-bellied, red-faced, dull-eyed cop who is too used to having everybody but drunks roll over when he says "Play dead." I see a cop who enjoys instructing the ones who don't comply. If the white letters etched in black plastic pinned to his shirt are to be believed, I see Officer Kuyek.

I think of the study done on policemen somewhere in California. The numbers bark for attention. Five percent were eminently suited to the job. They could handle the stress, they liked dealing with the public, and felt great about being a cop. Thirty-five percent were found to be totally unfit due to a variety of serious mental disorders whose symptoms could barely be alleviated, let alone cured. The other sixty percent were considered treatable.

These numbers are probably true of all the professions.

Pause for thought when searching for a dentist. But it's a weightier matter when the odds are screaming at you that you are dealing with a potential psychopath in a blue uniform accessorized with handcuffs, a club and a gun ... always the gun. I am alert.

"Lawrence Weilander?" he said in that endearing way cops have. Half question, half accusation.

"Nope." I am somewhat relieved, wondering at the same time what Slickie's been up to. Lawrence? So that's the secret name denied to us all these years, not even so much as a Larry to give it away. Hardly worth the effort and a letdown — like most secrets. You know, I let my dog lick me once, that kind of thing.

"Just call me Ace," he'd say in the vocal tone of a carnival barker. A short, snappy, "Hurry, hurry, step right up" voice that made us all call him Slick instead.

Officer Kuyek steps back and checks the number on the door frame. "Does Lawrence Weilander live here?" He asks, giving me the hard stare.

"Yeah. But he's not here."

"'Zat so?" Then he turned towards the street and it hit me that there were a few things wrong with this movie. Why only one cop at the door and not two, as you might expect this time of night? The other officer was still in the car talking into the cellphone partially obscuring his face. The car was unmarked, although they were both in uniform.

Fat Boy steps off to the side, points at me, and just in case the entire block wasn't awakened by his door-pounding act, hollers loudly: "'Zis da guy?" The cop in the car looks at me, does a double-take, and shakes his head no. All without removing the phone from his face. Not the first time I've been accused of looking like Weilander. Why, though, isn't the cop in the car on the doorstep since he's the one that knows what Weilander looks like? But I am at ease now with the chubbo filling the doorway. Clearly an order-taker, and his orders seemed to be to take Weilander. There was nothing personal when he asked who I was. Nevertheless I bristled.

"I beg your pardon?" Old habits die hard.

"I said what's your name?" And at this point I saw the good officer would like nothing better than to charge the barricade and trample all the little smartasses like me with his horsey's hooves.

"Cagney," I smirked, "James Cagney." Come and get me, copper. Come and get me, you dirty rat.

"Well, Mr. Cagney," beaming and triumphant that I had caved so quickly, "do you know the whereabouts of Lawrence Weilander?"

"'Fraid not, officer ... uh ... Kuyek," I said, squinting at his tag. "Or is it Kye — yak?" I am teasing the dog, inches away from the jaws of the slavering beast. He strains against the chain. Suddenly a link breaks.

A loud crash sounds out like an armload of dishes hitting the floor. This is followed by a muffled thud, a smaller crash and a cry of pain. Then footsteps move quickly up from the hollow of the basement stairs. Now what?

Ray heaves into view, a little red-faced, with his hair mussed up more than usual on one side of his head.

"Sorree," he says. "I tripped."

Officer Kuyek and I were both somewhat amazed; particularly since closer inspection revealed that Ray's tousled hair was actually the spread tail fan of a ruffed grouse. There were more feathers stuck to his boots and clumps of various bits of coloured fur clung to his clothes. Almost an improvement.

"Off to the powwow are you, Ray?" My clumsy chum. Discreetly I point to the tail feathers. Ray pats his head and carefully removes them.

"Whoops," he chuckles. "I'm afraid I've made a mess of Weilander's taxidermy stuff."

Cops have radar. Even the ones with double-digit IQs develop it. Like the way pigeons, not the smartest of birds, know if you're just walking past them or you want to kick their stupid, cooing asses into the next park. Officer

Kuyek, eyeballing Jimmy Cagney and Powwow Ray in the house of a guy he was looking for, was experiencing those telltale blips that told him something was very wrong. I could practically see his thought process and watched as three lemons came up and a buzzer rang. My own signals were wailing "ah-ooga, all hands on deck." I look at Ray. He knows what I'm thinking. We may have to abandon ship.

The cavalry came charging around the corner with tires squealing and a clattering tailpipe that shot out sparks as it dragged along the pavement. A vintage half-ton with the passenger door loosely wired shut lurched to a halt at the curb. Out jumped a grinning Weilander. Too late, as he suddenly realized, to prevent the cop in the ghost car from busting him. Typical. Fucking guy was always drawing heat.

Ray and I bobbed down the walk in Officer Kuyek's wake. His call-the-shots partner finished stuffing our felonius comrade in the back seat and got back in the car. He was turned away from me and talking to Weilander, but I managed to glimpse a gaunt, vulpine face with a thin mustache perched above his upper lip. He looked more like a long haul Greyhound driver trying to look like a cop, the kind that wear mirrored sunglasses and never smile. And he appeared vaguely familiar. Again, looking over his shoulder, he gave me the once over nice and slow, barely glancing at Ray.

"Brrrr," said Ray with a shiver.

"Caught that, huh?" I said quietly.

"Well, he seemed very interested in you. Who is he?"

"Fucked if I know. Maybe from the restaurant."

We stopped at the end of the walk. Weilander's face was screwed up in the gimme-a-break mode. He was waving his hands around — which was a good sign: no handcuffs. As they pulled away from the curb he suddenly remembered Ray and me and mimed the sign for telephone. I acted like I didn't know what he was talking about. Ray fluttered a wistful little wave good bye.

"I suppose," said Ray tentatively, "we'll have to ..."

"View this as an opportunity."

"An opportunity?"

"With a capital O, Ray. How much time do you figure we have before Weilander worms his way out of whatever shit he's knee-deep in?"

"Hmmm. Well ..." Ray ponders, holding his chin, thumb and forefinger, as we walk back to the house. Finally, he delivers his pronouncement, with all due seriousness and gravity. "Let's see ... allowing for travel time to and from the station. Juxtaposing ..."

"Juxtaposing?"

"Yass, juxtaposing the briefest of booking procedures with Weilander's tendency to be a little, um, talkative ..."

"Yappy, Ray. Bastard never shuts up."

"Okaay, yappy then. Um, I'd have to say anywhere from an hour to twenty-five years without parole. Depending."

"Let's just say forty-five minutes to an hour then, to be on the safe side. Lots of time."

"Time for what?" asked Ray, looking serious all of a sudden. Like he wanted to tell me something.

"Time for inspiration, Ray. Time for assistance from the magical world of botany."

I reached into my shirt pocket and pulled out a white, cylindrical, perfectly rolled joint. Ray's relief was evident, closely followed by a look of delight. Did the cops make Ray squeamish about the body, I wondered? Who cares? I needed clarity.

"I'm inspired already," beamed Ray, looking at the joint as if it were a chocolate éclair.

"It's only skunkweed, Ray. Hydroponic shit. That's all there is until the crop comes in."

"You always have the good stuff." Ray meant it and it was true.

"I think, fellow seeker, you will nevertheless be amused," I said. "But not in the house. This stuff is rank. Smell hangs in forever."

"Okaay, where?"

"Let's stroll over to the creek. There's a couple of things I want to check out any way. I'll just get the door."

"I'll go." Says Ray as he turns rapidly and chugs up the walk.

"Grab the key, then. On the table by the phone."

"Okaay."

I start slowly towards the bike path, counting the houses. Weilander's is the sixth from the galvanized barrier that marks the end of the street. At least one of the remaining five contains a dog — no, not a dog, according to Weilander, a hound from hell. "If you're going out and it's on the street, stay home," he said, totally deadpan. "Don't even think about running to the car unless you know you'll make it." I thought he was overdoing it a bit, kidding. All the same I looked for evidence: a "Beware Of Dog" sign, a nameplate with "Baskerville" on it, or torn scraps of postal uniform. I was also seeing if any lights were on in the living rooms and bedrooms I was passing.

chapter three

Standing in the umbra outside the splash of the last streetlight, I put one foot up on the bumper that sat like a steel eyebrow atop the pavement turning circle that dead-ended the street. Beyond, in the semi-dark, was a grassy plain which, until a few years ago, had been the old creek bed. Twenty yards across this sward the dike rose a steep fifteen feet. You'd definitely need to angle your way up if you were carrying something heavy.

And I could see the faint outline of a little path that did just that. Good.

Ray finally appeared on Weilander's front steps. He tried the door to make sure it was locked. Squinting and shading his eyes from the streetlight he shambled down to join me in the shadows.

"Couldn't find the key, Ray, or did you stop for another bite?"

"No. I had to take a wiz. Sorree. Here."

He gave me the key. I wanted to ask did he flush but couldn't quite bring myself to do it. I hoped for the best.

Together we walked to the dike, huffing and grunting up the steep pitch to the bike path on top. Below, on the other side, was the muddy channel of barely moving water. We found a patch of grass a few feet downslope and sat. Fifty yards to our right the long stretch of Elphinstone Street intersected and bridged the creek at right angles. From there the water flowed due west alongside a park, under Pasqua Street, past the airport, and out onto the prairie to join the Qu'Appelle.

Part of the Apocrypha of smoking marijuana is that you can pass a joint around any place, any time, with any number of people, in varying states of health, and never catch so much as a sniffle. I buy that. Even when the host sticks the entire joint in his mouth and moistens the outside of the paper by pulling it through his wet lips a few times. Such a classless thing to do, more for ceremony than purpose. Weilander is one of those guys. It's disgusting, but harmless. Nevertheless when I light up and take a couple of tokes and hand it over I say, "Don't slobber, Ray, if you can help it."

"I'll try." He makes a big slurping sound.

"Ha ha," I say, not amused.

It was good skunk. Very good. I'd be tempted to say great, except, being a purist, I believe you need real sunshine for greatness, not just a Gro-Lite. There is no scientific evidence to support this thesis. It verged on great, however, and after three passes I announced, "That's it for me. I'm sailing. How you doing, Ray?"

"Mmmm. My sufficiency is suffoncified."

I chipped the half-smoked joint. "We'll save the rest for later." Then I tucked the roach back into my shirt pocket.

"Mmm-hmm. Much later." Ray laced his fingers behind his head as he sunk back into the side of the hill, sighing dreamily the whole way down.

"Oh shit!" he said, sitting bolt upright like one of those inflated clowns you punch that pop right back up again.

"What's wrong?" I ask, looking all around, on high alert.

"Shit. Shit. Shit!" he says again, peering at his knuckles. There's a dark patch I can see on his hand. Ray delicately sniffs at it.

"Dog shit, to be exact," he says, pauses, and then with

mock seriousness, adds, "Thank god I found it. I might have stepped in it."

It takes very little to provoke mirth in this state. Both of us stifled snorts, trying not to make too much noise. After we relocated I lay back on one elbow and watched Ray rewipe his hand on a clean patch of grass, then, adding a bit of spit, on his pants. Collecting yet another hue for his palette of odours.

It was still warm. Soft, vagrant gusts of wind rushed in from the west, then faded. Tattered holes in the clouds were filled with stars. The half moon, partially revealed, horseshoed towards the horizon. *Media Luna*. Like the name of that funky little restaurant in Playa del Carmen. Balmy Caribbean January evenings. The joy of being unbundled and sensuous in a minimum of clothing. Snow, howling winds and forty-below did not exist. Like now.

I stretched out fully, consciously inclining towards the south. Crickets sang. I could feel the continent beneath me; stretching and curving, criss-crossed with the veins of creeks and rivers as it was a thousand years ago, pulsing and thrumming all the way to Panama. I could hear a rhythmic buzz becoming louder, interspersed with tiny whines. Ray the Relaxed was sawing logs, oblivious to the mosquitoes that had found us.

There was no use in wishing I still smoked tobacco, erroneously thinking it kept the little fuckers at bay. But I did. The wind helped, driving them off when it sprang up. But when it dropped they'd form miniature squadrons, lazily peeling off one by one as they drifted in for the kill. Whine. Slap. Squish. The Battle of Wascana Creek.

With the raging conflict for air superiority, and the sounds of Ray's industrial output, it's a wonder I heard the soft scrape of gravel on the path just above our heads. Say what you want about the effect of snarling dogs foaming at the mouth. Far more chilling is when they stand there, perfectly still, staring at you with beady red pinpoints for eyes. Not even panting, just drooling and licking their chops. Like this giant, the biggest Rottweiler I had ever seen.

I feel suddenly very exposed. The prairie will do that to you. I am on a slope in an essentially flat landscape, between a killer dog and a miasmic creek. I have no weapon. Not even a burning cigarette to at least take an eye out while I'm going down. Basically, I'm fucked.

"Hey, Ray," I say softly. His eyes pop open.

"Yaasss?" He says, lifting his head.

"You wouldn't have a spare T-bone on you by chance?"

"'Fraid not," he says, only slightly perplexed.

"Pork chop?"

"My, do we have the munchies!"

"Not exactly. But we may have a problem." And I motioned towards the beast. Ray turned his head just as it emitted a low growl.

"Oh," he says, "a doggie," obviously not taking Rottweilers as seriously as I do.

"No, Ray, not a doggie, a fucking devil hound!" I'm seconded by another growl. "This is probably the guy that chewed the rear tires off Weilander's truck."

"Oh," says Ray, unconvinced. "Well, I have my emergency jerky." He fishes around in his pants pocket and finally pulls out something the size of a cinnamon stick. He picks off a few bits of fluff and smells it. "Mmm. Not bad. Now I have the munchies. Are you sure?"

"For fucksakes, Ray, give it to the dog!"

"Okaay. Okaay. Here, boy." And with obvious reluctance he held out his foul, nitrate-laden snack.

"Careful, Ray," I cautioned as the dog lowered his head and moved towards him.

"Careful? Noo," says Ray in baby talk. "Not of doggie doggums. C'mere, boy. Have some snack. C'mon."

I watched, fascinated, as Ray waved his beef stick and the beast inched forward with delicate little steps. Not quite as graceful as a Great Dane stalking a squirrel, but balletic nevertheless. Finally, with Ray crooning, doggie got close enough to sniff the treat, which he did once, twice, and then snorted and shook his head. The dog would not eat Ray's jerky. No way. But in no time he was waggling his ass the way tailless dogs do, alternately licking Ray's face and deliriously sniffing his clothes.

"Close call." I say, relieved.

"Oh no. Doggums wouldn't hurt us. Would you. Boy? Noo." The dog's head tilted to the side.

"I meant the jerky, Ray. You almost lost your snack."

"You're right. Oh well, losers weepers." And he popped it in his mouth. The dog seemed to laugh along with us, then flopped down beside Ray. Even in the dark I could see those quizzical Rottweiler eyebrows, and the tongue lolling out the side of its mouth, resting easily on a serrated row of bone-crushing teeth. Ray the Beast Tamer casually scratched his ears. Then he scratched the dog's.

The mood had changed. Ray fussed over the beast. I sincerely hoped that Doggie Doggums was not going to be his permanent name or there'd have to be another murder: either Ray or the dog. I shifted to get rid of a pebble that was digging into my lower back. The pebble stayed with me and I realized the sharp pain in my spine was internal. The song in my head was a spiritual: "Glory, glory, hallelujah, when I lay my burden down. No more sickness, no more sorrow, when I lay my burden down."

Slowly, almost lazily, like the doubts that were creeping in, I watched a car drift down Elphinstone. Must be a drunk. They drive slowly with exaggerated care and wonder how it is the cops know to flag them. It made an abrupt left on 17th Avenue just before the bridge. One of the tail-lights was half out. Smart move getting off the main drag. Not too drunk to be cagey. I turned to Ray.

"Okay, I'll tell you how it happened," I said. Ray said all right, stroking the dog. "On one condition." I added.

"What's that?"

"No more Doggums. Get a name for that thing!"

"Why, I already have. I'm calling him Gandhi."

"Gandhi?"

"Mmm-hmm. He wouldn't eat the beef jerky."

"That was taste, Ray, not vegetarianism. You should call him Escoffier or maybe name him after the local health inspector."

"No, it's Gandhi. Besides he's a dog of peace. Aren't you, boy?" Gandhi looked up at Ray in utter devotion. You could almost hear him saying, "Yes, brother, I am peaceful ... to you."

"Whatever," I said. We sat for a moment. A light breeze had sprung up giving us relief from the bugs. I could barely hear a car idling somewhere. Maybe that drunk stopped to relieve himself.

"She OD'ed, Ray. Her choice."

"On what?"

"China White."

"Hmmm. That sounds interesting. How?"

"Well, here's the thing. I brought some with me. On my way here I ran into Moyer. Remember him?"

"Oh yass. The Wrong Reverend."

"That's him. Anyway he's into all that shit. Part of his exploration into 'alternate theology.' I had a sudden inspiration and asked could he get me some. 'The purest of the pure,' he said, 'if you think you can handle it.' Then when I saw her I knew I had to find a way to use it on the little cow. Get her loaded up and hope for the best. It wasn't seeming like murder to me ... just capitalizing on opportunity."

"So you weren't really trying to kill her," Ray chirped hopefully.

"Oh yeah, Ray. I wanted her dead ... or at least in some kind of permanent vegetative state. I don't even know why, except she really got to me. She was meeting me for the first time and didn't even try to make a good impression. This corrupt, stupid — and I mean willfully stupid — bitch was quite deliberately and carelessly rude to me. It wasn't even personal so much as she didn't care one way or the other. I could have been the janitor or a guy on a bus instead of her fiancee's father. She just wanted what she wanted. She simply didn't care what anyone thought, or whether they thought anything at all. It was like I didn't exist. It bothered Donald too, but she knew he would choose her no matter what the provocation. He had no power to resist. Even being so fucking stupid she knew that."

"Okaay," said Ray, softly, appeasingly. "I'm beginning to..."

"And her ass," I interrupted, "every time I looked in her direction she had it stuck up in the air, digging into this bag or that."

"That doesn't sound so bad," teased Ray.

"Believe me, it was awful. She wore these black tights and they were covered with little fabric pills, the kind that says she doesn't wash them all that often. She was like a scruffy, skinny, juvenile cat in heat. Meowing and rubbing up against anything that stood upright. It was hard to watch. And there was my idiot son, oblivious to all but his immediate needs, glowing with love. And that's another thing ..."

"What?"

"Never mind. It doesn't matter." But it did matter, it mattered a lot. As recently as yesterday, doubts had arisen as to Donald's paternity.

I considered talking to Ray about it, but I didn't get a chance. Suddenly the dog's head jerked up into the Sphinx position. He coughed a short wuff and stared hard in the same direction the drunk's car had taken. Canine hearing is as acute as their sense of smell so who knows what he heard? It could be anything, from a furry nocturnal creature in the tall grass to a hangar door slamming shut at the airport a mile away. Or — my guess in hindsight — the officious snick of a cartridge being chambered.

Gandhi growled as I shifted to get a better look, and something burrowed into the ground where my feet had been. At the same time I heard a pop and felt a sharp sting in my cheek. With the second pop a spray of dirt exploded between Ray and I. Adrenaline took care of the rest. I hollered that someone was shooting at us even as I clawed and scrambled up to the path and hit the ground on the other side. Despite a roaring in my ears every sound was magnified and in slow motion. I could hear the pebbles displaced by our feet making little tinkling noises as they settled. Two more rimshots on the snare drum — pop pop — were closely followed by the squeal of tires peeling out. That, but for a small groan and heavy breathing, was the end of the deadly percussive riff.

We stood slowly, patting ourselves. Doing inventory, brushing off dirt. "You all right?" I asked Ray.

"Yass," he said dreamily, "are you?"

"Yep." No embellishments. Nothing like a moment of abject terror to induce humility. Pilgrims at the end of a long journey, we were saved.

I stood for a second, then squatted at the brow of the hill and shivered in a post-adrenal spasm. Ray walked down to inspect the inert, shadowy form of our saviour. He crooned as he ran his hands over the dog and was rewarded with a groan and a half-hearted attempt to raise his head. Ray then picked Gandhi up as if he were a pup and cradled him like a baby.

"Let's take him back to the house," he said.

Quietly we crossed the grass and up the street to Weilander's. Under the streetlight the dog's head was a bloody mess. I felt a little ashamed that I had never liked Rottweilers very much. This guy had stood his ground while Ray and I were scrambling.

I unlocked the door and Ray carried the dog straight to the bathroom and put him down in the old clawfoot tub. The toilet seat was up and I reached over to flush the yellow liquid in the bowl. Ray looked at me.

"In case he needs a drink later," I said.

"Your cheek is bleeding," said Ray.

I looked in the mirror and got the usual shock: seeing a much older guy staring back at me. More salt than pepper in the hair and beard, albeit more neatly trimmed and shorter. No grey ponytail for this kid. Making a statement with your hair is for the young or celebrities or the trying-too-hard. The lines are etched more deeply and I finally have the Marlboro man crow's-feet that I thought would make me look more distinguished. I had a small puckered wound just below my right cheekbone with a drying trail of blood running south to my jaw. Kind of a handsome devil though, I thought, in a hollow-eyed sort of way.

I cleaned up and watched Ray, astounded by how thoroughly he washed his hands before attending to Gandhi. He was fiddling with the hand held spray extension that passes for a shower when the phone rang.

"Now what?" I snapped to Ray, beginning to wonder if this night was ever going to end.

"Yass," said Ray. "I think he's going to be all right, aren't you, boy?"

Doggie responded with a single, high-pitched note forced through his nose, an ultrasonic whimper.

I walked to the living room. Maybe it was rifle guy calling to ask me if I'd step outside for a moment so he could try again. Is this for real? Could someone actually be trying to shoot me? It was not really possible. It hit me that it would be gross understatement to say that much had happened since dinner. My life had been one of measured and familiar turmoil until today.

The old cut-and-run manoeuvre beckoned seductively. All I had to do was ditch Ray, the dog, the bundled bitch in the basement, unplug the phone, finish my business errand and then I could go back to being peacefully morose, dying faster than I would like, and hiding out in Toronto. Fuck it! I picked up the phone.

"Hello," I answered, trying to sound groggy.

"At last, you prick! Where the fuck have you been?" It was Weilander.

"Hey, Slickie, you sound a bit tense."

"Tense! I've been calling for half an hour, for chrissakes. What are you guys doing over there?"

"Getting some air. What's up? I thought they were going to throw away the key on you."

"No way. Listen, you gotta come and get me."

"Now?"

"Yeah, now. Before they get back."

"Before who gets back?"

"Just come down to the station and get me, willya? And hurry."

"Yeah, yeah. Okay. Relax."

"Just do it quick, eh." Click. Dial tone. Just like that.

I had a brief conversation with the back of Ray's head while he ministered to Gandhi. Then I left, out the back door this time, down towards the creek again, then across the east-west alley to the next block where I had parked the rental car. I only rented one this trip, and it was in my name, since I had no deliveries to make. I suppose I could have even parked in front of Weilander's house.

I snorted, remembering Ananah's bitching about the long hike — slurring her words, staggering. I practically had to carry her up the walk. She hadn't smelled good. Her unwashed, thin blonde hair shrieked for shampoo and she reeked of booze and tobacco smoke. Oh well. She was going to smell a lot worse now.

chapter four

Taking the long way to the station I cruised over to Elphinstone, then slowed past 17th Avenue. There was nothing in that first block where I had seen the car with the busted taillight. Weilander and I could take a closer look on the way back from the station. If there was a way back.

There was almost nothing to like about any of this. What little amusement Weilander's discomfort provided was offset by the thought of rows of beady red eyes lining the shelves; those gleaming incisors waiting in the dark for me to reach for the cheese. The rat I smelled was not Weilander. Intentional betrayal was not in his nature. Unfortunately, his mouth had a tendency to operate independently of his brain. And he wasn't all that sensitive to begin with. Your darkest secrets could tumble out at the most inopportune moment if you had been foolish enough to confide in him. Because of my nature I knew — before the argument in my mind was wisely resolved in favour of not going — that I would go. I had to see if Weilander, master hunter of great repute, was being set up as a Judas goat.

When the lights at the south end of the Albert Street bridge — appropriately beside the stone cottage where I remember two ladies who resembled Gertrude Stein and Alice B. Toklas, at least in spirit, used to live — took half an hour or so to change from red to green, I realized that I was still soaring, held aloft by the power invested in tetrahydracannabinol and the sundry other compounds inherent in the hydroponic marvel that Ray and I had shared; so I had to remember to drive faster, with less skill, in order to remain inconspicuous.

Weilander was one of the first guys, one of a handful, to embrace the dawning of the Age of Aquarius. This crowing bantam rooster, this plucky runt of the litter, this wiry little big mouth rolled up his sleeves, tipped his bowler over one eye and sashayed down to Haight-Ashbury to see first-hand what all the fuss was about. He was back in the fall wearing the sleeveless poncho vest that would define his sartorial style for well over a decade. It was his only memento from an eight-hour attempted penetration of Mexico that ended in deportation by a squad of federales who were thoroughly disgusted by his lack of dinero. But it was a tale of senoritas, cervesas and souvenir stalls until the badges showed up.

Throughout a particularly long prairie winter of unrelenting cold he regaled us with tales of his "summer of love" in San Francisco. One fuckup after another reduced us to snickering puddles. On occasion he'd have a rare supply of marijuana that we'd buy in nickel bags and hold tremulously over the toilet bowl, ready to flush, each time we spotted a strange car in the alley.

That was a long time ago. Now I realize that Weilander and I share a great deal of history. A constant undertone of competitiveness and rivalry, fostered mainly by him and encouraged by me, makes us more like brothers or close cousins than friends. Which explains why I ignored the paranoia as I entered the cop shop on my rescue mission. The things we do for family.

Those lights in the back room, the ones they shine in your eyes to get you to confess, had all been moved to the front lobby. This called for sunglasses. Instead I kept my driving glasses on, putting at least one layer of smudgy obfuscation between my dilated pupils and the observant world of the desk sergeant. Too bad they were almost clean. Another layer of dust and eyebrow grease would have helped me feel less exposed. I resisted the urge to tap dance as I walked over to the counter.

The odour of charred hemp wafted up from my shirt pocket. Too late to leave it in the car. Then the desk guy's head came up; he looked straight at me, his piercing black eyes glowering above the ridge of high cheekbones. Grow his hair shoulder length, wrap it in a headband, and you'd have Sitting Bull. Actually, you'd have Standing Bull. I was staring at Robert Nakahoot and I knew for a fact that he was over six five.

"Hey, Frank," he said, smiling slow.

"Robbie! Holy shit they got you too. They catch you in that uniform you'll be here forever."

Robbie was polite enough to laugh at what was an old joke between us. Then he reached over and enveloped my hand in his catcher's mitt.

"No, just a few more years and I'm outta here. Good to see you, Frank. How you been?"

"Not bad. Better, I gather, than Weilander."

"Oh yes, our Slickie has the wrong people mad at him."

I could see he was concerned. Then he peered closer, thinking hard about something. He asked what I was doing tomorrow afternoon. I stammered an excuse he brushed away. He was telling me we needed to talk. I found this curious — a lot of water had passed under our particular bridge — but I didn't say anything. He wrote a number on the back of a card telling me to call him around two. So I did the Toronto thing, saying, yes, of course, I'll phone, when I had no intention of doing so.

"Where is Weilander anyway? Do I have to put up money for the bastard?"

"No," he grinned. "I'll go get him. He's in an interview

room. Didn't want to sit out here in the open while he was waiting."

I watched as Robbie told a younger cop to take charge of the desk for a minute. "Yes, sergeant," he said, practically saluting. There was respect in the kid's manner, not fear. I would never have figured Robbie as a cop, but I knew he was one of the five percent totally suited to the job. It would have been good, getting together with my old teepee mate. Maybe I'd finally confess about that night with Brenda. Blame it on the openness fostered by mescaline. In the meantime, I had a body to dispose of, people were shooting at me, and I wasn't exactly making my living the old fashioned way. Another time perhaps.

I could hear the chafing irritant known as Weilander talking his way down the corridor. The rare bass notes were Robbie. They hove into view, a small coyote running ahead of a giant wolf. He made a beeline for me.

"Let's go," he said, and over his shoulder, "Thanks, Robbie."

"Yeah, thanks, Robbie." I half grinned as Weilander dragged me to the door.

"Uh huh," he said. "Call me tomorrow. And maybe you better think about getting a new blade for your razor." Pointing to my cheek where I could feel the newly dried blood. "Or was that just a close shave?" Then he leaned over and sniffed the fumes that rose, almost visibly, from my shirt pocket. "Mmm. New cologne?" His eyes registered more than a slight amusement. He knew something was up, the bastard.

"C'mon. C'mon. C'mon," yapped Weilander.

Robbie watched from the front steps as we hurried out to the car. I waved as we drove past but maybe he didn't see me. He just stood there, not moving.

After a couple of blocks, a long time to be silent for some, I looked over at Weilander. He was half turned checking the traffic behind us. There was none. I looked at his serious expression, at his droopy, red-rimmed, wet-brown, mournful eyes, and burst out laughing a second or two before he did.

"So?" I said, probably more relieved than he to be out of there.

"So, nothing," said Weilander. "It's a personal thing, I guess, between me and that fucker, Shpak. Jeez, I'm just happy Robbie was on duty, eh. I owe him one."

"What was their excuse to pick you up, then?"

"Questioning. Said I resembled a suspected something-or-other. All bullshit. That fucking prick. Robbie caught them trying to run me past the desk and stopped them. He looks at me like he doesn't know me. Says, 'Are you here to volunteer information, sir?' I don't wanna be here at all, I say, going along with not knowing him. 'Right,' he goes. And then he turns to Shpak and that fat fucker and says, 'What are you doing here? You guys are off duty. I better not see you put in for overtime.' So they give me the hard look and leave. Fuck, I thought for sure they'd be waiting outside."

"Like they don't know where you live."

"Fuuck," he said, like it just dawned on him. And now I have an even bigger problem. I would probably have an easier time dumping a body from a room at the Sheraton than from Weilander's basement.

"Why is that cop after you, Slick? What have you been up to?"

"Don't you know who that is?" he asked, somewhat incredulously, then added darkly, "He knows who you are."

When he said that I got a queasy feeling in the pit of my stomach. It was accompanied by a perfectly rational terror. This could mean one of many things, none of which held promise. The shit is up to my armpits and heading for my chin. I still couldn't place the cop.

"That's Roger Shpak. You know, Dagmar's boyfriend."

So that's the ex-wife's latest paramour. Go figure. How could I keep up, especially since I wasn't living here any more? All I knew about Dagmar — a.k.a. "The Dragon", or, in Donald's case, "Mummy Dearest" — was that as she started to age it was getting harder for her to dazzle the boys.

"Man, that's a mean looking guy, Slickie," I said, sucking air through my teeth.

"You got that right."

"Her dog must have died."

Weilander laughed and told me yeah, the weird psycho shepherd with the wild stare did die. Poisoned a day or so ago. How did I know?

It was an informed guess meant to be a joke. I explained her penchant for strays, big vicious ones that were loyal only to her. Some kind of power thing you could make a career out of trying to figure out. They never seemed to stick around for long, though. Maybe she thought a nasty cop would last longer.

"Jeez, you could be right, eh. How come I never noticed that?"

Because you're blind, like all the others, I thought. The numbers may be dwindling, but the stupidity level appears to remain consistently high. There was even a cast of hangers-on waiting in the wings, watching leading men come and go, hoping for their big break — even the family doctor, an otherwise intelligent man, if a tad shy on ethics.

"Oh I am right," I said, "but the cop won't last very long."

"Ya think?" Said Weilander, perking up.

"Sooner or later she finds another stray junkyard dog and the guy is toast." Then, after a nicely timed pause, I said, "Unless ..."

"Unless what?" he asked, like a jackfish diving at a silver spoon. It never ceased to amaze me, this power she had over certain men, like she had radar for their particular deficiency, to be the knight that rescued her. More amazing was their proclivity to treat me as some kind of informed and sympathetic confidant — even to the point of asking for my advice. And how they would hang on my every word when I talked about her, shocked yet secretly pleased by my irreverence.

"Unless he treats her like shit. That could prolong things a bit."

Poor Weilander, practically the only one of my male friends or relatives that Dagmar hadn't slept with. I knew it bothered him. After she and I split up many years ago, she started picking them off one by one. Except for Slickie. I don't think she did it to torture, or get even with me. No, she had Donald for that.

"Bastard's playing around on her," Weilander said somewhat glumly.

"Does she know?" I asked, already figuring the answer.

"She does now," he said, his sad face tinged green under the street lights.

Knowing Weilander as I do, this part was only too clear. It was like a geometry theorum. Pi, or the devastation of the information, equals 2 'r' squared; or, the sensitivity of the issue times two, squared by the most inopportune moment of divulgence. Classic Weilander blurt.

"Gee, I wonder how she found out?" Weilander completely missed the irony in my voice.

"Well, I ran into her at the liquor store. Fuck, she sure likes the good booze, eh? Two bottles of Glenlivet, a Courvoisier, and she's still shopping. I could see she was a little down and I figured it was trouble with her old man. I mean, I saw him with Janey at the bar, off in the corner by themselves. What was I supposed to think? Hey, do you know her? Janey? She's got one leg shorter than the other or something. Very pretty though."

"No, I don't think so." Weilander looked over and caught me smirking.

"Aw, fuck off," he said, "I know what you're thinking. Do you wanna hear this or not?"

"Do I have a choice?"

"No," he said, laughing at himself in such a sweet way that he would always be forgiven.

"I think I know how this one comes out anyway."

"Well, how was I supposed to know?" The blurter's lament. "She looked sad. All that booze and no party. It's okay, I say, he'll come back. 'What do you mean come back?' she says. 'He's dead.' Dead? I says. Jeez, he looked pretty healthy at the bar last night. Musta been awful quick. 'At the bar?' she goes, 'Who are you talking about?' Your boyfriend, I say, that cop guy. 'Oh that fucking cocksucker!' she says. Whaddya mean, I go, who were you talking about? 'Satan,' she says. 'He's dead. Someone poisoned him.' She's talking about her goddamned dog, eh. And then she sorta dragged the rest outta me."

I laughed outright at that, Weilander saying, "What? What?" the way people sometimes will.

"So that's what it's about. The cop is pissed off you told on him."

"Yeah, sorta."

"There's more to this?" I asked. Of course there would be more. There would always be more when blind opportunism encounters chicanery unbound.

"Well, I went over to her house for a drink. I mean, you know, I hadn't seen her for a while. Holy shit, she was really knockin' 'em back. Since when is she such a big drinker?"

"I don't know. People insist on telling me about it but I haven't seen it first-hand."

"When's the last time you saw her?"

"Five or six years ago, at least."

"Oh." And this seemed to make his telling me all this okay, like he didn't have to tiptoe around my feelings. A rare moment of sensitivity for Weilander, albeit misplaced. It was mercifully brief, and irritating, too, but I let it all slide.

"Yeah? And?"

"Oh yeah. So we have a few drinks. Well, she had a few, I had one. And the next thing I know we're on the couch, going at it hot and heavy, when the door crashes open and there's Shpak standing there. Man, I nearly shit myself. He had his uniform on. Jeez, I thought I was having a flashback, eh. 'Take a hike,' he says. 'No, you just stay where you are,' says Dagmar. Then they start screaming back and forth. 'He stays...He goes...He stays...He goes.' Fuck, they were still hollering when I left."

"Pretty bad timing," I said, quietly marvelling at the impromptu set-up.

"You got that right."

"So when did all this happen?" I asked.

"Just before you got here."

"You figure he's done with you now?"

"Hope so. He's pretty pissed off. Told me to stay away from both of them, Dagmar and Janey. Greedy bastard. Jeez, I was nowhere near Janey anyhow. I mean, she's a nice girl and all but she could hardly keep up on a hike through the bush."

There was the Weilander I knew. Sensitive as a frozen lug nut. In truth his career as an ecologist/ornithologist kept him out on the prairie, and he did like to take women along unless it was hunting season. Dazzle them with nature talk, get free labour and a warm place to sleep. A practical man, he needed a two-legged woman.

"Hey, where ya going?" asked Weilander as we shot past our turn.

"I want to show you something," I said, fishing out the roach and handing it to him, still not sure about how much to divulge. As little as possible, for sure.

I mulled it over as I drove west to Pasqua St. where I would turn south to 17th and then cruise east to Elphinstone. Elephant stoned, as we used to say. After a three-match effort he got the roach lit and offered me a toke. I waved it off, already exactly where I wanted to be. Efficiently he reduced the final third of the joint to a glowing pinpoint pinched between his thumb and forefinger. Then he dropped into a little gob of spit at the tip of his tongue and gulped it down.

"Aaaaaah," he sighed, settling back, closing his eyes,

letting the warm air rush in through the window and wash his face. "Good shit. Skunk?"

"Yep."

"Nice. Now, if I just had a cigarette. Times like this I miss them."

"Giving proof to the assertion that marijuana does lead to harder drugs."

"You got that right. Must be the inhaling sets me off."

"How long since you quit?" I asked.

"Almost two years. You?"

"About the same. I get the urge after I toke up, too." Then, after a pause. "And about ten times a day, every day, on top of that. Or every time I see someone really enjoying a smoke. Or when somebody is smoking my old brand. Or going around a corner in the morning and catching a whiff of some office clerk in a doorway. Or when I dream about it. Or especially when one of those colourless, geekoid, prohibition Nazis makes one of their self-righteous speeches. Or when I talk about it, like now, with another pathetic addict like yourself."

"You through?"

"I guess. Except to say that other than that it doesn't bother me a bit."

As I listen to Weilander's laugh echoing my own I'm reminded of how our differing approaches to smoking dope often lead us to a similar place.

When I toke up I like to dive into the cosmic soup and stay submerged, while answers to ancient riddles drift by and attach themselves to fragments of the day. Abandoning myself to the undertow, as with certain types of music, I can sometimes get beyond words, past all reason, down into the cleansing void. Then, spiralling up through the double helix of a Bach fugue, in a swirl of rising bubbles, I burst into the light and bob on the surface like a beatific bell-buoy Buddha.

Weilander is already there, contentedly afloat, astride a makeshift raft, pointing to a multicoloured fleet of sundry craft. Hallooing and waving to every errant thought that crosses his bow. Chatting to anyone who cares to listen. Inviting them all to tea. But, as Lao Tzu says, "The surface and the core are essentially the same."

It seemed a shame to cut the party short. However, it was time to enlist the considerable expertise of my bird-hunting master. On the prairie or in the bush Weilander was a very tidy guy. All business, and focussed like a blowtorch. I could picture him in a coulee looking for a wounded grouse. Moving quietly back and forth, never talking, he would methodically comb every square inch of ground until he found it. He would not lose a bird willingly. It was waste, inefficient, and he thought of the bird, too, suffering unnecessarily. Now that he was stoned he'd be even more intense. Time to put Slick to work.

chapter five

The five-block stretch of 17th Avenue runs straight from Pasqua to Coronation, where it takes a dogleg south and traces the creek back to Elphinstone. I pulled over in front of one of the stuccoed bungalows that shared the south side of the avenue with ranch-style houses in wood siding. Across the street was sidewalk, grass, and a stand of old willows lining the creek.

"What's up?" Weilander questioned me as I pulled over and parked.

"You are," I said. I held his arm with both my hands and steered him like a granny to the wooden footbridge that crossed over the channel to Turtle Park.

We stood leaning on a rail in the middle of the bridge. I told him what had happened to Ray and me while he was trying to call us from the police station. I didn't mention Ananah. Looking down at the water, the half-eaten moon had rippled edges in the wake of a passing muskrat. We could just make out its head at the point of the V, making for the bank with a mouthful of goodies and taking its own sweet time.

Weilander listened, punctuating my description of events with "Fucks" and "No ways" until I finished giving the blow-by-blow of the attack.

"Jesus H. Christ," he snapped, "this is serious. A Rottweiler, eh? Just how big is it?"

"Big," I said, somewhat annoyed. "The biggest."

"And it's still in the house?"

"He was when I left, but that's not the big picture here. Besides, Ray has everything under control. The dog seems to like him."

"Ray! What the fuck does Ray know about dogs? What do you see in that guy, anyway? Ray. Shit. All he knows about is how to eat."

"Right now I'm wondering what I see in you."

"Sorry, man. I know Ray's a good guy. It's just dogs and me, you know?" Then, hopefully: "Hey, you said he was shot, right? Probably not too frisky right about now."

"Probably not."

"Four shots, eh, and two were together, bang bang?" Showing he was paying attention. Taking charge now.

"Yep."

"Bangbang?" He asked, running the two bangs together. "Or bang bang?" Leaving some space between the two.

"Bang. Bang."

"So what does that tell you?" he asked, smugly, master to student.

"Oh, I dunno," I said from the back of the class. "That someone is trying to kill me?"

"No." Sternly. "Think!"

"Okay. Someone's trying to kill Ray," I said, not exactly playing dumb. Who knows what he was driving at? I expected a slap from his deerstalker cap or a poke in the ribs with his Meerschaum. Instead he smiled grimly and pressed on.

"Or the dog," he said, cutting the next one off at the pass. And then, as if hit by a revelation, "Wait! Jeez. It could be the dog. Someone's been offing them for months now. It's in the paper."

"Someone is killing dogs?"

"Yeah. Mostly Rottweilers, too. And some shepherds —

guard-type dogs." He thought for a moment. "It'd be the first time one was shot, though. Usually they're poisoned. Couple were lassoed and hung. Wouldn't eat the food."

"Jesus," I said, disgusted, completely ignoring my most recent venture. That was different, though. People deserve it. Dogs don't. Some people, that is. "That's sick!"

"It sure as fuck is," Weilander agreed, regardless of his feelings for our canine brethren. "Anyway, where I'm going with this is, what kinda gun?"

"You mean like a rifle or pistol?"

"Nah. Pretty much had to be a rifle. Not a hundred percent, but pretty much. What I'm asking is what type of rifle? It seems to me that the two together were too fast to be bolt action, see, but not fast enough to be semi-automatic."

"Ah," I said, playing along. "You're thinking pump."

"Right!" he said, pleased. "I'm thinking pump. Sure, it coulda been a semi, and whoever it was just took their time, but usually a guy squeezes off a double he does it in a hurry."

I happen to know that Weilander's deer rifle, like his shotgun, was a Remington pump. So I figured this was why he was on the pump kick. I also figured he was full of shit. There's no way you can tell a pump from a semi-automatic just by hearing the shots. But as long as it was keeping his head in the game who cares?

"And this tells us what?" I asked.

"It just tells us what it tells us. One piece of information."

"Oh. And to think I just wanted to try and see where the shooter was standing. Maybe find a clue."

"Let's go," he said, "I got a good idea about that." And without so much as a flourish of his cape or a "Come, Watson, the game is afoot," he at least pirouetted and strode quickly down the creek in true Holmesian fashion. Moriarty awaits.

"Ouch."

"Sorry."

"Fuck, you're clumsy."

Weilander came to an abrupt halt just as I caught up to him, creating a minor slapstick moment. So at his suggestion we split up.

"One of us should check along the creek," he said, meaning me. Since he didn't offer a choice, I knew, from a hundred times hunting with him, that he was onto something. Otherwise it would have been: "One of us goes this way, the other guy goes here, which one do you want?"

"Okay, I'll take the creek," I said, just like in the bush, confirming that he was in charge like he needed to be. Out of gratitude and respect I would not challenge him. Just about everything I know about upland game birds, a fair bit, I first learned from Weilander.

I had pestered him for over a year before he introduced me to the mysteries. "I don't go hunting with anybody who hasn't been out before," he would say with finality, "not even you."

So I borrowed an old single-shot twenty gauge and went grouse hunting with Buddy, a transplanted draft dodger from the States. Most of that day was spent diving for cover as he shot at anything that moved, which, on the prairie, meant everything but the fenceposts. Buddy, having outkilled me, three gophers and what surely must have been a sparrow to nothing, was magnanimous in victory. "Don't worry," he said, a Cinemascope grin cutting his face in half, his arm squeezing my shoulders in a testosterone-fuelled hug. "Y'all'll get the hang of it."

Weilander's second pronouncement about hunting was, "Nah, I'll pass. I never toke up when I'm hunting." He was not as resolved on this, reconsidering a few minutes later: "Well, maybe a coupla puffs wouldn't hurt." Bingo. After that it was just a matter of asking the right questions to provoke a dense, thorough and peculiarly Weilenderian dissertation on the wildlife of the northern plains.

I learned, first by lecture, in the cab of a half-ton, then empirically, how a chicken sits just inside the trees soaking up the sun, conserving energy, facing the wind for a quick take-off; where a ruffie is at any given time of day; how Huns like the corners of a field where the harvested grain spills; why you gotta get on a pheasant quick; how to be ready for the staggered flush; how to lead them when shooting on the wing; and about slitting their crops to see what they're eating.

Along the way I became relatively adept at finding and securing birds on my own. I'd be one of the guys you'd want to go out with. Or, considering recent developments, maybe not. Hunting humans in a non-warfare, non-genocidal, non-ethnic cleansing sense would be an entirely different matter. I have no experience there. Well, very little. The herd could certainly use some culling, no doubt about that. Even if it were indiscriminate we could do without one or two less geniuses anyway; particularly the ones with new and improved formulae for rocket fuel. But not by hunting.

With a certain crowd people-hunting might be more popular if it weren't against the law. I used to wonder how people could possibly hunt others for sport? Indians, like the Beothuk (or even more recently in San Salvador), are a prime example of the human animal being treated like game. Truth is, since I've started hunting I've met some guys who could do it; I've seen a haunted bloodlust in their faces as they cruise the same fields I do, looking for coyotes. All it would take to get them to shoot fellow humans would be to make it a legal sport and they would fire away without the slightest tinge of conscience. Scary guys, and in some sort of weird corollary, I know that if they were dead the world would instantly become a better place.

It is against the law, however, and flowing from that is a lack of camaraderie. Any kind of partner would be a potential neon arrow pointing in your direction. "He did it, your honour. I tried to stop him." Making people into accomplices, like Ray — and soon maybe Weilander — is a good stalling tactic but it's eventually unreliable.

So we're looking at a solitary occupation here, which

fine. It's not, however, a game for everyone. ..ainly not for the sick fuckers who would really do it, the ones who sublimate by hunting bears and wolves and coyotes. No, these guys need to brag about it, and even lie when necessary. "That head, the one above the fireplace? Oh that's the V.P. of corporate finance for Widget Telecom. Tough bastard. Got him on a smoke break during a human resources seminar." What really happened is that they found a homeless guy frozen solid out by the garbage and cleaned him up before having him stuffed and mounted.

The biggest drawback for these guys is that they themselves could be hunted. This would, as it were, eliminate at least ninety-five percent of them. In absolute truth the idea of any species hunting their own kind for sport is truly repugnant. What other species would do it?

Take Ananah. It wasn't sport. Nor was it violent. Or well-planned. It was opportunistic and karmic. Like how Robbie told me the Indians used to hunt. Except they had more respect for their quarry. And I mean used to hunt, before they were infected with European civilization. I went out with a group of guys from the reserve once, and it was like an anti-safety film. What not to do while hunting. I couldn't count the number of times I'd look behind me and see a rifle, with the safety off, pointing at the small of my back. On the whole, if you were to give him a machine gun and a pocketful of grenades, I'd rather go hunting with Buddy.

The male sharptail grouse is a dancer. Mostly he hangs in flocks and although we hunters call him and his tribe "chickens" he is not the true prairie chicken. He likes to dance at dawn; same time, same place, every day. This instinct is so strong that if you build a barn on that spot he'll dance on the roof when you're done. And you see his style reflected in the actions of powwow dancers replete with bustles, top knots and ankle bells. Tailfeathers and rump in the air, he keeps his head low to the ground and whirls and turns on the flattened grass of the communal lek. Pitty-pat, pitty-pat, always forward, weya hiya, weya hiya. Circle left, circle right, weya hiya. Keep that head low: bob, bob, bob.

They're hard enough to hit with a shotgun. And if someone's been at a particular flock, even once, they get wilder and more wary. A raised eyebrow will send them up in an explosion of wings that will raise the hair on the back of your neck and give you a quick queasy feeling in the pit of your stomach. Off they go calling in a cacophonous, high-pitched gobblegobblegobblegobble. Somehow, drawing a bead on them, you're never quite ready for the second flush of a smaller bunch that has hung back — solely, it seems, for the purpose of distracting you from the first group. Divide and conquer.

On a more primitive level it goes like this: "Crash, startle, whirr, hackles rise, see birds. Oh yeah, hunt. Getting away. Aim quick. Focus. Focus. Crash. Startle again. More birds. Closer. Others too far now. Switch to this group. Switch! Switch! Getting away. Fuck. Gone. No. Don't shoot anyway. They just get wilder. Watch where they go. Follow. Try again. Fuck. Fuck. Fuck."

When they're really wild they'll fly forever. Forget this flock. But even if those sharpies just go a little way they will now post a sentry or two in the trees, right at the top. Look carefully and you'll see a black bulge on the skinniest part of the trunk, high up, a vertical take on the snake that ate the hat, which suddenly sounds the alarm if you get too close. This time they will fly out of sight. Tough birds to hunt; near impossible when you're using arrows.

So, as Robbie told me after a day or two of quiet observation lying in the tall grass beside the dance ground, we make our move. Before dawn we take slender stakes about a foot long, to which we have fastened simple loops of sinew that close like a noose. We plant these at random throughout the lek with just the loops showing. We slide back into the tall grass and wait. At dawn the dancers arrive. When it is time to leave, a few are left behind, having bobbed low into the waiting snares. We pray: "Thank you, brother, for sacrificing yourself to feed me and my people. Tonight I will dance as you have danced to give you the honour and respect you deserve."

In similar fashion, minus the element of respect, I sat Ananah on the couch. She watched and seemed to perk up as I unfolded the small rectangle of paper and dumped the entire contents of white powder on the glass of a framed photograph of Weilander holding a dead sharptail.

"This is the shits," I said of a chopped-down plastic milkshake straw. "I'll go get something better." Then I pointed my finger at her and said, very emphatically, "Now you wait and don't take any of this until I get back!"

"Ew. No way. Sure," she said, a sly look brewing under the hooded lids of her goat eyes. "I'll wait right here." As if she was in any kind of shape to go anywhere else.

I was combing along the creek not knowing what I was looking for when Weilander went, "pssst." He beckoned me to join him by a clump of tall bushes halfway between the creek and the sidewalk.

"This had to be the place," he said. "Take a look from here." And he pointed towards Elphinstone Street. I looked past the streetlights and into the shadow on the other side. You could just barely make out where Ray and I had been sitting.

"Be easier to see with a scope," Weilander said. "And I found this." He was holding a shell casing between his thumb and forefinger, looking very pleased with himself.

"A clue," I said.

"Fell right outta this bush," he said. "No wonder they missed it." Then he pushed the bushes back with his forearm. "Check this out. This is what I was looking at when the casing fell."

He was pointing at a set of footprints in the soft loam under the shrubbery. Boot prints, not shoes or runners, smallish; and one was in front of the other in what you might call a shooting stance. I shivered involuntarily as I looked at the tracks. Somehow the shell casing and the boot prints made it much more real and terrifying now. And the big question is, who would be shooting at me and why?

"You okay?" asked Weilander. Concerned.

"Huh? Oh yeah," I said swallowing the last of the panic. "Hey, nice work, Sherlock."

"Thanks. You know what's odd, though?" He handed me the brass casing. "This is a two-forty-three."

"So?"

"So not a lot of people use this calibre. Hard to get shells. Most guys like a light gun go for the two-seventy. Out here anyway. The only one I've ever seen is mine."

"You mean," I asked, "the shooter used a two-forty-three pump and you're the only guy you know has one?"

"I guess."

"Well then, let's check the tread marks on your shoes and we can wrap this whole thing up."

"No kidding," he laughed. "Fuck, it's weird, eh?"

"Weird enough," I replied. Even so, I couldn't help a surreptitious glance at his feet despite knowing that the prints under the bush actually had a tread; as compared to the thin-soled, round-heeled, cracked-leather, bargain-basement, Army and Navy specials that Weilander habitually wore.

"Well, Slick, if this had been a presidential assassination attempt you'd be up for the big promotion."

"Hey, I guess I would," he said, quite pleased with himself. "Does this mean I get the girl?"

If I had been drinking something it would have sprayed out everywhere. As it was I sputtered. I knew he wasn't referring to Ananah but it took a moment. Then, I wanted to say, "You're too late, pal, she's already been got." Instead I went with, "Be careful lest you get what you wish for, my friend." Getting an idea for a joke I would never play. He'd be really surprised if — no, don't go there.

"Yeah, yeah," he said. Then, wryly, "Guess we won't be calling the boys in blue, eh?"

"Now why would we need the Leafs?" Clowning, I came that close to telling him the whole story.

"Piss off," he laughed. "You figure it's them, don't you? Shpak and the fat boy?"

"Except for one thing."

"What's that?"

"How did they know Ray and I would be there?"

"Hmmm. I dunno." He thought for a moment. "Maybe they came back to the house and you were out. Or they coulda driven by and spotted you."

"Maybe." Not convinced and now wondering how anyone could possibly have known where Ray and I were.

"What then?"

"Nothing. Let's go see Ray."

"Oh boy," Weilander said glumly. Then he muttered to himself about never letting people stay in his house, ever again.

I thought about leaving the car and maybe just walking back, but Weilander was already off and running and I tagged along, the usual step behind.

chapter six

"**H**ey, slow down there, Lawrence."

"Who?" Weilander stopped in mid-stride. "You know I hate that name."

"Actually, I had forgotten all about it until Officer Kuyek brought it up."

"Fat prick," he sighed. Then, with the reluctant maturity that comes with age — whether you want it or not — "Aw, who cares anymore? It was my dad's name, eh. Like he couldn't spare me one of my own, you know? I tried since I'm a little kid, but I could never do anything right for that guy. It was like I was always letting the name down or something. Man, it's been a long time since I thought about that." He paused for a bit then snorted, "It's all mine now, though. May he rest in peace."

"At least it isn't some kind of hinky name like Helmut or Ralph," I said.

"I wish," he laughed. "I coulda lived with that."

"Still," I said. "Not such a big deal."

"My dad was a big man, and not just because he owned the hardware store in Rat Knee. I didn't ever tell you about him, did I?"

"As a matter of fact, you did," I said. (More than once, I thought.)

Lawrence Senior was a red-haired, freckled, bulky, six-footer; like his twin daughters, Weilander's sisters, younger than he by a year and taller by four inches. Slickie was small and dark like his mother.

The defining moment, at least the one Weilander most frequently dwelled upon, was a day when he was eleven or twelve. Either Glenda or Lenore had tied the family dog to the tailgate of their truck, and dad backed over it. That afternoon he took his kids hunting for the first time. Glennie, the oldest twin by twenty minutes, bagged her first duck. Lenore whimpered with her eyes shut when the gun went off, and Weilander, who "didn't have the goddamned sense to look after the goddamned dog properly," was sent to retrieve the bird. "Okay, Dad," he said. And without a thought he waded into the weedy slough that was chest deep to him and brought back the duck. "By God, you might just be good for something after all," said Dad.

On the way home Glennie sat up straight and beaming beside Dad in the cab of the half-ton. Lenore, bored, pouted in the corner by the door. Weilander, wet and muddy, rode in the back with five dead ducks, each of which he had retrieved, feeling strangely happy. "After that at least the bastard took me hunting," Weilander would say. "I was the best bird dog the old man ever had."

"Why don't you just change your name legally?" I asked on the two-minute drive back to his place. By then I had pretty much decided to let Ray help me explain the body if it should happen to be discovered by Weilander.

"You can do that? I thought it was just your last name you could change."

"Nope. You can change any or all of however many names you have. Become Mallard S. Duck if you like."

"Fuuck," he said softly, staring off into space, thinking of the possibilities. "You know, I might just do that."

Sometimes we don't think of the obvious until it whacks us in the head with a shovel, I thought as we coasted into the parking spot behind Weilander's truck. Better there than in front of the house.

Suddenly — bam — it hit me. A brilliant flash, a bolt of lightning. The solution — no doubt provoked by all the reminiscing about Weilander's early adventures with ducks. In the way a word or two will gel out of a jumble of thoughts, the phrase "foul play" — from 'fowl' of course — swam onto the view screen of my cogitometer. Not to be out-revelated by Weilander, I too had an epiphany. Sometimes the obvious is indeed elusive.

Bathed in the glow of self-wonder, I contemplated the possible, calculated the probable, and applied the litmus of cold, hard reason to the results. Bing, bing, bing. It came up cherries every time; the only clear, clean, non-toxic solution to the Riddle of the Bundled Babe, my own personal mystery. It was also, naturally, the simplest. The truth shall indeed set us free; and the truth is...

"Oh no," came the mournful lament from a Weilander who had been reluctantly dragged from his reverie. As was I from mine. "It's him. Stay in the car."

"Who?" I asked, quickly scanning the street.

"There!" He said, pointing to a small, white, four-legged form perusing the walk with its nose. Slowly he prowled his way to the steps and raised his head to tentatively sniff the air while looking, seemingly, at Weilander's front door. Probably getting a whiff of Gandhi. Or Ray.

"This is the dog you warned me about," I said, knowing the answer would be affirmative. "I thought it was the Rottweiler."

"Oh yeah. This is the dog," said Weilander. "And if I could figure out where he lives I'd poison him myself. Probably immune, the fucker."

"This thing between you and dogs goes back a long ways, eh Slick?" He just turned and looked at me.

"Okay," he said, "you go out there."

I took another look as the dog trotted stiff-legged down the walk towards Weilander's half-ton. I noticed the thick neck and shoulder muscles and the wide, oddly-proportioned head. He stopped suddenly and stared at our car. In the headlights his eyes had a pinkish, albino-like cast and a stare blanker than Ananah's. This was a dog inured to influence; as remorseless as addiction.

"You couldn't pay me enough," I said. We both laughed. I shut the car off and we sat there watching the beast from the pits of Hell sniff Weilander's curbside tires and calmly raise his leg and piss on them, both times stopping to first look straight at us. Then he turned and rooted his back legs in our direction before sauntering off towards the creek. All we saw was a stubby tail, a puckered asshole, and an enormous pair of balls delicately mincing back and forth as he trotted into the dark.

"Let's get this guy, Slick. I'll help. We should at least be smarter."

"Yeah? Well don't miss. I gave him a couple of good whacks with a tire iron and it hardly even slowed him down. Hey, did I ever tell you about that, how he chewed through my tires?"

"Just a few hours ago. Remember?"

"Oh yeah."

We sat. It seemed like a very long time but was probably only four or five minutes. I was feeling calm now that I knew what to do about Ananah. It really was so simple. Foul play. There were no signs of it unless Ray bruised her up taking her to the basement. There couldn't be. She did herself in. She just OD'ed. Obviously, I felt some guilt — which is why I couldn't see it before. All we had to do is just leave the body somewhere neutral. If Ray and I had taken her down to the creek and left her there it'd be all over now. A bit close to Weilander's maybe. But maybe not. A lot of people use the bike path.

She must have been a cute little thing of one or two when her daddy left. Little blondie with the sky blue eyes. Did she laugh then or was she born without a sense of humour? She hadn't exhibited any that I could see. A function of stupidity I assumed. When Donald told me her dad was a fundamentalist Christian psychiatrist who worked for the navy I inadvertently burst out laughing. I thought he was putting me on.

Talk about being buried deep. I could see a team of divers working in shifts at bone-crushing depths, in numbing cold, with underwater torches and jackhammers, trying to pry open the bathysphere anchored to the ocean floor. Even with eventual success all they would find would be another face-plated metal ball with its door riveted shut. He'd be a tough guy to get through to.

This, I am informed with a straight face, is Ananah's "abandonment issue." If you ask me, she caught a break early. Donald's mother, Mummy Dearest, also has abandonment issues. Only it was her mother that left when she was three. Apparently, she was schizophrenic — which would make her easier to get through to than Ananah's dad, but you'd need a program.

Ananah's mother, Jackal Woman, kept her until she reached puberty and then dropped her off in Christian boarding school for four years while she went to Africa to find herself. In a curious bit of symmetry, or not, little Dagmar was also sent away to boarding school during her long metamorphosis into a flying, fire-breathing, killer reptile. Her dad, who was too old to be a Nazi war criminal, was an avuncular, cherubic artist with a regional reputation and a charming German accent that had everybody fooled but me. "So what if they didn't have Nazis back then, you don't think they had war criminals?" I'd say when I was feeling foolish enough to vie against forces far larger than I could safely contend.

Out of the blue I am now Donald's "abandonment issue" and it doesn't feel like a promotion. The term is new to me, but then I don't watch a lot of daytime television. A year after all attempts at reconciliation had failed, and a year in which I had my face washed almost daily by yet another Dragon mate, I finally went walkabout for a few years before returning to the prairie. At no time was I ever out of communication or unavailable to Donald, so I can see where the "abandonment" part can be a broad-based term.

I have dealt with the source of this attack and with Ananah gone that neutralizes Jackal Woman and just leaves me, as ever, opposing the Incendiary One. Man, am I sick of this game! The dark nourishment of guilt is a richer feed for some than for others. When this is tidied up — soon, I hope — like Chief Joseph, "I will fight no more forever." In the meantime, if I could ever get his attention, I'd like to tell Donald that the two of clubs is the two of clubs: find a way to win with it.

"Whaddya say, Slick, shall we make a break for the house?"

"Yeah, fuck, why not? But I'm going to feel like a can of Dr. Ballard's with legs."

"More like a bag of kibble. Ray figures Gandhi is a vegetarian."

"What?"

"The Rottweiler. Ray calls him Gandhi. Says he's a dog of peace."

"He does, does he?" Weilander said, shaking his head.

He got to the steps first, but waited for me to open the door. The first thing I saw was Ray sitting in what was once called an easy chair. The room was bathed in the light of several different vintages of lamps. Ray had an odder than usual look on his face; at peace, in a wild-eyed sort of way. He had the fire, in ancient terms, and we were welcomed to it. Gandhi lay at his feet, a turban of gauze bandage wrapped around his head; quite alert and staring at Weilander, who had gasped "Holy shit" when he saw the dog.

At right angles to Ray's chair was the couch and barnboard coffee table. Upon it lay a purse. Shit! How could I have forgotten that? The larger mystery by far, however, was a velvety portrait of a matador draped across the back of the couch. Could there be two of those? My mouth dropped open. I looked over at Ray, who was coyly staring down at Gandhi's turban. Then, from the bathroom, I heard a distinct and definite flush.

The toilet bowl coughed its last gasp and the tank began filling with a noisy sigh. Each sound was magnified to me. Taps could be heard turning on and off in the sink. The floorboards creaked. I felt dizzy.

"Hey, who else is here?" chirped Weilander, happy to still be in one piece.

I was staring so hard at Ray that the dog yelped. Who indeed?

"Well, you two are just in time," Ray said, a bit too heartily.

"In time for what, Ray?" I asked quietly, trying to get his eyes to stop dancing around the room to look at me.

"Pizza! It should be here any minute." He was pleased, like it would solve everything.

"Great," said Weilander. "Fuck, I'm starving."

He bounded to the couch, forgetting all about the dog who, in any event, seemed quite chilled out. All he did was gingerly sniff in the direction of Weilander's pant leg while Weilander leaned over, as if to pat Gandhi on the head, then thought better of it, and settled back. He was absently trying to straighten out the matador on the back of the couch when the bathroom door opened slowly, creaking like a tomb.

A bleary-eyed, groggy Ananah staggered into the room. She was mopping at her face with a grey washcloth, festooned with dark blotches. A black smear ran down one cheek.

Even though I knew it had to be her, I was stunned.

"Well, hello there, lovely," said Weilander, spreading his tailfeathers just a little.

She stopped abruptly and squinted in his direction as if peering through a gauze curtain.

"Ew," she said. "First the creepy guy with the dog and now yew. Like, who are yew guys?"

Any relief I might have felt at finding her still alive vanished with her remarks. Ray had probably saved her life. At the very least she'd still be wrapped up in the rug and suffocating without some kind of help from him. Ray just looked away. Weilander laughed.

"This is my house," he said, "if that helps you out any."

"What would help is if yew'd hand over my purse," she demanded, as if it were being held hostage. "My gawwd. I'm a mess. What am I dewing here?" And then she spotted me, still speechless and leaning against the wall by the front door. "Oh yeah," she said, trailing off, trying to blink a thought into place. "Yeww brought me here." Then, "Oh yeah, now I remember." And a conspiritorial grin appeared on her face. Or perhaps it was gas.

"Jeez, I'm not interrupting anything here am I?" Weilander cracked, giving me a certain look. Wiggling his eyebrows. For a second there were two people I wanted to kill. I glared at him, much to his amusement. Ray seemed a bit squirmy.

"Give her the purse," I said, "so she can finish cleaning up." Weilander handed it over to Ananah's dryly snapping fingers.

"Then I want to talk to yew about something, Daddy," she said to me as she snatched the purse. "Yew know?" And she attempted a wink which, in itself, qualifies as incitement to mayhem.

"I told you not to call me that!" I snapped.

"Oh, did yew?" She said indifferently, fearlessly. "Well yew are about to become my father-in-law."

Not if I can help it, I thought, still resolved. I'd rather enter a long-term relationship with a toothache. But I said nothing as she clunked her way back into the bathroom.

Weilander was grinning away with a mouthful of wisecracks he barely managed to keep to himself. He sat with one ankle on the opposite knee, jiggling his foot.

"Any minute now, eh, Ray?" he said.

"It should be here already," said Ray, feigning

annoyance. Just knowing it was on the way was enough. Food was coming. He was not a guy to panic if the pizza was a little late.

I really needed to talk to Ray but, since I also needed to regroup, it could wait. I couldn't think anyway. Too much noise. Too many people. A room at the hotel was looking better and better. She's alive. Fuck.

Weilander grabbed the phone on the first ring. The place was beginning to seem like a circus. No doubt the acrobats were calling to say they'd be a bit late. He wandered around the corner, trailing the cord into the kitchen, talking quietly, listening a lot.

"Jesus, Ray," I said, alone with him at last. "What happened?"

"Wherever I start, it will be a long story," he cautioned. "And I am a bit low on energy."

"You'll talk after you eat, is that it?"

"Okaay," he said, as if it were my idea.

"I can hardly wait, my friend. But I can tell you this; I liked that girl a whole lot better a couple of hours ago."

"Me too."

Weilander finished his telephone conversation with an audible, "Okay, okay, relax. I'm coming over." He brought the phone back into the room and said, "I gotta go out again. That was Glennie. All fucked up about something."

"I thought she lived up north now," I said, remembering that she was just as prone to blubbering as her sister.

"She's down to pick up the kids. They spend summers with Kenny, her ex."

"She at Lenore's?"

"Yeah."

"Better take a box of Kleenex."

"You got that right."

Glennie and Lennie, Weilander's twin sisters from the planet Lachrymosia. Each of them were quite tough in their way; Glennie, physically, being tall and rawboned; and Lenore, mentally, being only slightly less taller and more rotund. But when they weren't being all hard-assed about something they were weeping, or about to weep, or looking for an excuse.

Because of a tiny bit of history between Glennie and me — miniscule, really — and a vague feeling of unease regarding Lenore, I tended to avoid both of them.

Ananah exited the bathroom having made an effort at cleaning up. Nothing short of doing laundry was going to help her aqua cotton vee-neck top. The pills on her black polyester tights would survive anything but fire. She had Tammy-Fayed more dark goop on her eyelashes, to contrast the pinkish splashes on her cheeks. Some shiny, pale, putrescent shade of lipstick outlined rather too boldly with a brown eyebrow pencil made her look like she'd just had some chocolate milk and forgot to wipe off the moustache.

In her platform sandals she walked like a cross between Lady Frankenstein and someone condemned to forever climb stairs. Her hair was neatly parted but still limp. She appeared more alert, flushed, but seemed to have developed a sniffle and kept wiping at the corner of her nose with a bent forefinger. I hadn't moved from beside the front door. She tottered towards me and, just past the couch, her purse slipped out of her hands and fell to the floor. Slowly, she bent over, legs straight and slightly apart — like a Vargas girl — to pick up her stuff and put it back in the bag. Ray modestly turned his head. Weilander stared in wonder. She stood up and sauntered over to me.

"Yew wouldn't have any more of that stuff, would yew?" she asked softly.

"No. You took it all, remember?"

"Whoops," she said, being cute, one finger on her lips. "Sorry about that." Then, "D'yew think yew could get some more? I'd be very grateful."

Whatever perfume she had spritzed on couldn't mask the sourness wafting up from her body. It was making me queasy.

"Okay," I said, "I'll get more, but not now. It'll be my gift to you, but ..." and I lowered my voice even more, "you mustn't tell anybody about it. Not even Donald." Only this time I'll get the real stuff, I thought, right after I have Moyer's legs broken.

"Sure, no problem, I won't say a word," she lied. "Um, when?"

"Not tonight, but soon." It couldn't be soon enough, you little bitch.

"Ew, I can't wait," she said, quickly followed by, "Hey, that's not all, is it?"

"What do you mean?"

"For my wedding present ... I mean, mine and Donald's."

"Oh no," I said. "Be patient. That will be a big surprise."

"Ew, I love surprises," she squealed.

"Well, I think we're all going to enjoy this one," I said, already formulating a more foolproof scheme.

From the look on Ray's face, I might even expect some help from him next time. He brightened considerably, however, when the doorbell rang.

chapter seven

The light was all wrong. It shot through a broken slat in the cheap vinyl venetian blinds and seeped in around the edges. Superheated dust motes danced, swirling and rising up the shaft, occasionally flashing pinpoint rainbow explosions. It should have been paler, the shadows not as sharply defined: the room a little gloomier, cooler. Less the brassy young harlot, more the tired old whore.

My watch lay on its side, at eye level, on top of a pizza box on the coffee table. Upside down and backwards it read 12:05, five after twelve. The one-fanged snake of my dreams poked up through the ancient middle cushion. There was a crick in my neck, and my lower back ached. I was waking up slowly. A river of unconsciousness still flowed only an eye-shut away. A sour, half-remembered, stale perfume odour intruded like smelling salts and shocked me into realizing that I was using the velvet matador as a blanket. I kicked it to the end of the couch.

I had been dreaming about Glennie. What, I could no longer remember. Except in the dream it was the young Glennie who, during a time more brief than an arctic summer, blossomed into a rare and fragile beauty that held for a few days and then withered and dried, on the thickening stem, with every passing glance.

Of the two sorts of redheads she was briefly the extraordinarily beautiful kind: long, slender legs that swelled into a perfect ass, skinny hips and a small waist sliding up smoothly to alabaster breasts with raspberry nipples. That first glimpse on the tundra, with her in funny little boots, a short dress with tiny roses, looking over her shoulder with a sparkle in her eyes, catching you in a moment where you ached to touch her, to run your hands over her, was just that — a moment.

A week or so later, after staggering home from the bar to my one-room apartment a couple of blocks up the street from Donald and his mother and Uncle whoever, there was a knock at the door. Glennie had followed me home. In a perhaps forgivable lack of judgement I let her in.

How could she not know? I mean, with sex, don't both people have to be there? How could a moment of alcohol-induced intimacy be such a tedious chore for me, and a life-affirming experience for Glennie? All I remember is that her three-week blossoming period was irretrievably over. Her breath smelled bad. Not foul, as in halitosis, just bad in that it was her natural smell, and always would be — just as I would always find it vaguely offputting and unpleasant. For her it was a shining moment according to the glazed, goofy look in her eyes and a disgustingly tender cast to the awed half-smile that played with the freckles at the corner of her mouth. I hope they were freckles.

How could she not know that my feelings for her, at best neutral and wary, respectful that she was the sister of a friend, had taken a plunge towards revulsion? I finished as quickly as I could. I didn't care where she was at, I just wanted to get away from the smell of her. How could she not know, not feel it?

I rolled off her and left her on the rug that she assumed was chosen in abandon but in fact was a ploy to keep her scent off my bed. I dressed quickly, wondering how fast I could get her out the door and on her way. How could she not know how absolutely stupid I felt allowing this to happen?

"Listen," I said, watching her hook up a tattered brassiere, "I have to be up early and I have to get some sleep. I'd ask you to stay but ..."

"I know," she said, an indulgent grin on her face and eyes positively wet with admiration. "I have to go too. But, my god, do you have any idea how beautiful you are?"

"Yeah," I said, "I do." Sadly, I did. I could see it written all over her face.

About the only thing I felt for Glennie now was irritation. Seven years later I ran into her at Weilander's second or third wedding. She left Kenny with her two kids and dragged me out to the patio. All moonie-eyed, with no encouragement from me whatsoever, she declared I was her lost love. It was like I didn't exist really; certainly my feelings didn't enter into it at all, and her family was on the other side of the door. I didn't even try to mask my disgust and I think she finally got it because I haven't seen her since. As to the content of my dream about her, who fucking cares?

The house was quiet, empty. Weilander gave Ananah a lift on his way to Lenore's. Looks like he stayed over. Ray and the dog were gone. It took a while to discover what had happened, and Ray's account is still a bit sketchy. He knew Ananah was alive when he carried her to the basement — and probably before that. He let it slip that he has medical knowledge of some depth, but was evasive regarding how much. I thought the bandage on the dog looked professional. Ray, more of a mystery than ever, and Gandhi, who had somehow assumed inscrutability, were still there when I shut my eyes for a minute and ended up crashing out on the couch. I don't know how long they stayed.

Sometimes, like now, in that state before fully waking, perfect sentences are formed. Word after word drops correctly into place. Problems are solved with such offhanded ease that even the "Eurekas" are muted. The success rate, however, for nudging these solutions into daylight is dismal. It's like carrying a brim-filled basin of water across a kitchen floor, trying not to slop over. With every spill a piece of the puzzle is dissolved. In Ananah's case, The Dilemma of the Undeceased Daughter-In-Law, the linoleum was awash.

In one sense and one sense only, it was good she had survived. From the moment I rolled her up in the rug I experienced feelings that definitely need examination. If I felt any remorse at all it was not during the episode, and certainly not for her. She had no redemptive qualities that I could discern, though I have long believed that redemption is always possible.

Perhaps in a photograph, or properly airbrushed on the page of a magazine, the sight of her could set you dreaming, trigger whatever response that comes when you see a lithe young beauty clothed in something erotic. She could have value in the abstract, as an object. Places where you could capture a certain expression, where she could not speak, where you could minimize the goat-like eyes. When Donald first described her she sounded great. He didn't see her as unclean, peremptory or joyless. I'm sure he saw mostly the repetition of small ecstasies. There is redemption in that.

When Ananah was dead I felt a certain exhilaration, a focus I hadn't experienced since my early days of hunting. But it was a surreal version of that feeling; not the same thing at all. The shock of seeing her walk out of the bathroom wore off quickly. I was not disappointed to see her, nor was I pleased. However, some things within me had been stirred; things I need to understand fully. I know that, for a time, it was dangerous to be around me.

That needs to be addressed.

After a bowl of cereal I sat at the table wondering if I wanted coffee badly enough to use Weilander's mouldy, grounds-filled, campfire-blackened percolator. The yea's took a narrow decision. I scrubbed it out knowing that the coffee was going to smell a whole lot better than it would taste.

Let's see, I chuckled to myself as I put the perk on the burner, who shall I kill today? Whoever it is, I'm going to need some work on my follow-through.

I could feel the heat creeping through the streets and alleys to surround the house. It was going to be a scorcher. I don't hunt any more, but I still get stirred up at the end of summer. In a week it would be duck season; two weeks after that, upland game birds, and sometime in the first week of October a residents-only season would open for the Machiavellian ring-necked pheasant. Donald's wedding was scheduled for mid-September, halfway between opening days for the ducks and the grouse, two weeks from today.

In the meantime I could see out the back window that the sky to the west was the washed-out blue of a summer intent on lingering a while. The light was a force in the cloudless sky, enveloping everything but the odd black hole of shade. Maybe I'd give Robbie a call after all. Declare a holiday, a day off from thinking about all this shit. Might be a good day to drive out to Rowan's Ravine. Have a swim — algae or no algae. Cruise the grids on the way back and look for birds. See what was on Robbie's mind.

The kitchen window was cracked open and I helped it the rest of the way to catch the last of the breeze before it died. I went back into the living room to raise the front window and get a cross-draught happening. They'd have to be closed again soon to keep out the heat. But for now the place needed to be aired.

I opened the slats on the blinds and froze. I'm fucking busted now, I thought. Because there, like the Bismarck, bristling with armament and steaming up the walk with a bone in her teeth, was Dagmar, Mummy Dearest, the Dragon. Now I knew fear, wild and unreasonable. Flight was my first response but my knees were water. Should I hide? What if she had spotted movement at the window? How about not answering the door? Then I remembered the time she knocked at the door of my little apartment looking for Mandy Mack.

Mandy was an art student who boarded with Dagmar. She was a quiet beauty — not nearly as timid as she initially appeared, although Dagmar treated her dismissively, called her a mousy little bumpkin behind her back, and gave her a break in the rent for babysitting. Anyway, in what could be misconstrued as a bit of payback, but wasn't really, Mandy and I were lying in post-coital slumber late one Sunday morning. Well, I was sort of dozing, half-listening to Mandy talking to my penis, asking would it mind if she gave it a name, introducing it to her finger, having little conversations back and forth. It was such a stirring chat that it was urging me awake. The knocking, sudden, loud and violent, intruded like a thunderclap.

"Frank! Frank, open the door. Is Mandy there? I know she's there, the fucking little bitch. Open the door!"

She knocked and pounded and kicked while Mandy and I lay in the twisted sheets like Hansel and Gretel, paralyzed with terror, not daring to move. "Frank, open this door right now. I know you're in there. I can see your feet, you cocksucker. Open the fucking door!" I looked down at my feet, then over to the keyhole in the door, and saw that it might be possible she could see them. My toes especially felt exposed and started to burn. Mandy, who suddenly seemed to be having a lot more fun than you might expect, threw a sheet over my feet.

Finally, as Dagmar was giving the door some prodigious boots, someone down the hall hollered they were going to call the cops if she didn't stop. "I know you're both in there, you fuckers!" She screamed. "You'll be sorry." And then she left, having cursed and pounded for an eternity. And it wasn't over — this being Sunday, my day with Donald. I was due to pick him up in an hour. "She must have found my note," Mandy said.

"What note?" I asked.

"Well, I left a note and a cheque in lieu of notice. I moved out yesterday. But how did she track me here?" she wondered aloud, shining in her innocence. Oh dread.

The breeze blew softly through the window, ruffling my hair. It would be the only affection I would receive today. There are no small battles with Dagmar. Any slight disagreement is either airily dismissed or immediately puffed up to Gulf War proportions. And it must be something very serious indeed for her to be out in the unflattering light of noon.

Stifling my inner coward I opened the door when she was halfway up the walk, a pre-emptive strike that slowed her down a bit. She was doubly startled to see me standing in the doorway. That answered one of my questions. She was expecting to visit Weilander.

"Well, well, well," she said, recovering in a heartbeat. "Jesus Christ, would you look at who's here. Decided to come to the wedding after all, did we?"

"Hello to you, too," I parried. "You're up early."

A peremptory hug with air kisses concluded our salutation. Her back felt dry and bony, slightly rounded under the lavender cardigan that covered her shoulders and arms. As ever, she dressed in layers — like the veils of Salome. A slip peeked out from under the hem of the oversized, old-fashioned sundress she had probably shoplifted from the Goodwill. Her legs, which showed from mid-shin to sandalled feet, were defiantly hairy.

"Mmm, is that coffee I smell?" she said a little too sweetly, almost as if she were polite.

"Yeah. C'mon in," I said. "Weilander isn't here though."

"What a thing to say!" she huffed. "Of course I want to talk to you. My god, how long has it been?" Bat, bat. Blink, blink. She was being coquettish in a grotesque way.

Her makeup, which she normally slept in, had been plastered on thickly. And if she fluttered her eyes any more assertively the lashes might stick shut. I admonished myself for thinking that way. Let he who is still youthful, paunchless and wrinkle-free cast stones. Were I one of my sisters I would no doubt be reaching for a Number 7 trowel myself. Most days, I could probably use a little blush anyway. It's just that I think a modicum of restraint is best.

There was something hidden under the Fauvist daubs, something eating her that wasn't due to the ravages of time. I am not going to get sucked into whatever it is. Keep it light, no matter what.

"You're looking good," I said, leading her to the kitchen.

"Why didn't you answer my letters?" she asked. Starting maybe.

"Um, well, I'm still thinking of how to respond. What to say." A quasi-lie, since both missives were about a wedding she knew I was struggling with, and, intentional or not, were loaded with insults and provocations that I was trying to rise above. Time to change subjects.

"You're right, though, it has been a while. I'm trying to think of when."

"Don't you remember?" She sounded hurt. "It was at that cute little restaurant of yours."

"Oh yeah," I said. "Wasn't that the night you tried to get the busboy to drive you home?"

"What?" she said indignantly. "I didn't do that. How can you say that, you bastard? Jesus fucking Christ."

"Just kidding," I said, thinking of young William; tall, skinny and fresh-faced. Georgie and I teasing him until he insisted one of us walk him to his car in case she was waiting. I poured coffee and put cream and sugar out.

"Well aren't you a riot." She fished around in a large, quilted bag. Out came a pack of menthols, a lighter and several individually wrapped candies that she bought in bulk from the health food store. Oh no, the dread conversation kit. I was in for a lengthy one, unless I could find a way to cut things short. Have faith, I told myself, desperation will find a way.

"Where's the ashtray?" She asked, delicately holding the cigarette at the end of her fingertips, blowing a plume of smoke at the ceiling.

"I don't know," I said, conveniently forgetting the one in

the living room with a couple of roaches in it. "I'll get you something."

"What, you aren't smoking these days? Jesus Christ, I thought you'd be the last one to quit."

"No, I think you're the only one left who smokes, Dagmar." Handing her a saucer.

"Lots of people are smoking," she said defensively.

"I mean us older people."

"What? Older! What a nasty fucking thing to say." She was protesting too much but I said nothing. I did grin.

"Oh, I get it. Very clever, Frankie boy, but I'm not falling for it." Then, in a far sweeter tone: "Now you wouldn't happen to have a little something to put in this coffee, would you?" Again, she tried to look demure.

"They say the eyes are the first to go," I said, pointing to the cream and sugar.

"Fuck off. I mean something to make it more interesting. A bit of brandy. Maybe some cognac."

"Not unless you want some oxidized Italian red. A tad early, isn't it? Doesn't the sun have to be over the garage roof or something?"

"Just for taste, for god's sake," she snapped. "Fuck, you didn't used to be such a wimp. Never mind, I think I have something." She fished in her purse again, pulling out a half-filled pint of decent Scotch. Unselfconsciously she sipped and poured, and sipped and poured again. When she put the bottle back it was only a quarter full.

"Ahh, that's better." She sighed, settling back a little, trying to get comfortable on Weilander's retro chrome chair.

About the only thing you could taste through the licorice candies and the menthol tobacco would be paint thinner. The serendipitous positioning of the table in the middle of the room, at least made it difficult for her to lean her chair back, sparing me from the panty flash, a routine that usually rode in tandem with the conversation kit.

"My god, these chairs are terrible," she said after trying

to get comfy. "I'm practically sticking to the plastic. Let's move to the living room. Do you mind?" she said, gathering her things. "It's cooler in there anyway."

Not waiting for a reply she swept through the doorway and made for the couch. She had both hands full, one eye shut, and a butt dangling from the corner of her mouth. Step into my parlour and all that. I followed through the mixed grey fog of cigarette smoke and gloom that trailed behind her.

She dropped onto the couch as lightly as a tick. The pincers of a major chatfest were tightening. Settling on the middle cushion she brought her legs up and crossed them like a kindergarten yogi. Then, with an expert flick acquired through decades of practice, she snapped the hemline of her dress so that it billowed up above her knees to expose her thighs and crotch in a brief display. It was Dagmar's signature move. It was why she wore dresses. While your eyes instinctively tracked the movement she studied your face with the cold impartiality of a scientist, attuned to every nuance of expression. Under this intense gaze — Did you flinch? Were you excited? Uncomfortable? — she would get to know you better than you could imagine.

Pantywise, this was a fairly major flash, say seven out of ten, which denoted the impending onslaught of some heavy conversation. Talk, after all, is a perfectly acceptable four-letter word for intercourse. Even without the lubrication of whiskey she could render your ear into a submissive pink pulp. I'll have to cut her short and run the risk of being rude and uncaring, have my rebuttal rebutted and so on until enough conflict had accrued to scratch her itch. Best to meet it head on. Get it over with.

"Well looky here," she snorted. "You do have an ashtray after all. And what's this?" She held a roach aloft for the jury to see, then dumped it and the rest into the saucer so she could have the ashtray that befits a lady.

"Jesus Christ, Frank, I thought you'd outgrown this shtuff."

"Shtuff?" I jumped at the gift.

"What?" She said, her brows furrowed.

"You said shtuff instead of stuff."

"No I didn't! I didn't say that."

"I'm afraid you did."

"I did not! What a liar. Jesus fucking Christ. What is this? You're jusht — just — trying to annoy me." In a flurry, she unwrapped another licorice and popped it in her mouth. It was followed by another cigarette. Subduing the offending orifice, she took a deep slurp of her coffee.

"Bastard," she added, only she lisped it around the bulge of sweets in her cheek so it came out "bathtard", showing me it wasn't her slurring her words — it was the bonbons. Nice try. I wondered how many drinks she had knocked back before venturing out.

"I have to go out at two, by the way," I said, deftly inserting my agenda.

"My, my," she said, recovering somewhat. "That'll give us a lot of time to catch up after all these years."

"Well, if I had known you were coming over..." I trailed off, not saying, "I would have paved the walk with broken glass." "Besides, you're here to see Weilander anyway."

"That doesn't matter, for fucksakes. Jesus, Frank, it's been six years at least since we've talked. Your son is getting married in two weeks and you haven't even responded to the fucking wedding invitation, let alone answer my letters."

"Did you respond to your invitation?" I asked, ever so softly.

"My invitation? I don't have an invitation, for god's sake, I'm his fucking mother!" One second, two seconds. She got it on three. "Ahh, I see. So that's what this is about. Poor little Frankie," she baby-talked. "Is his feelings hurt?" Mockery comes easily to her. It provokes and torments people.

I looked at the crumpled shroud at the end of the couch, then back at her.

"You know," I said in a kindly, smiling voice, "you'd look great in velvet. Something in a matador pattern, perhaps."

"What? What the fuck are you talking about?" Her annoyance stemming from the fact that I hadn't bitten.

"Well, I thought the invite was sent for fun. Show me what they looked like. I thought you guys would just assume that I'd be there."

"Oh," she said, her sails sagging, momentarily silent while awaiting more wind.

"I mean, why would you think otherwise? After all, I am Donald's father, aren't I?"

chapter eight

The last refuge of a scoundrel is tears, not politics; at least with this scoundrelle. Big wet ones, preceded by a furious blinking and overall moistness around the rings of goop that circle her eyes. I am almost embarrassed for her, such transparent ploys not being up to Dagmar's usual standards for subterfuge. Her timing was okay — we had reached an impasse — but her execution was sloppy, to say the least. Give her a three point four, out of the medal round.

A significant amount of civilized behaviour consists of stifling involuntary reflexes. We are not elk. There will be no attempted mountings on the subway platform, no matter how fetching the rump. Nor will I respond to Dagmar's indicated distress. As a matter of fact, it's a luxury to see a woman cry and not have to care about what's wrong. With this woman anyway. My dispassion gives way to annoyance as I watch her soldier on through the performance.

She rifles through her purse, apparently unsuccessful at finding whatever it is she's looking for. Hard to believe there wouldn't be at least one of everything in there. She dives in again, and again comes up empty handed. Her nose has grown and taken on a reddish hue, a neat contrast to the dark rivulets of mascara etching twin channels through the powder on her face — and quite a sacrifice for her art. She looks straight at me and, somewhere down deep, finds comfort in my amusement. As if on one level we're both glad I didn't get sucked in.

"Why it's Bubbles, the clown," I say.

She teetered for a nanosecond then fell to laughing along with me. Why not? It was easier, more fun, and not so hard on the makeup.

"You are a fucking prick, Frank. At least get me a Kleenex or something."

"Sure," I said, having seen several in plain view when she had churned through her bag. Now would be the time.

On the wall in Weilander's kitchen, placed so you could see it from the living room, was a poster framed in aluminum and glass. It was mostly black with splashes of red and small print in white; a great reflective surface, better than a storefront window. It showed Dagmar turn to make sure no one was watching, then make a quick move to the unshrouded end of the couch where she stuffed something between the cushions. She still had the moves, perfected by stealing cans of lobster, in the supermarkets of our student days. I grabbed the paper towels.

Dagmar dabbed a few smudges here and there, blew her nose and dropped the debris and the roll of towels on top of the empty pizza boxes. A quick check with a hand mirror led to some minor touchups and equilibrium was restored. Another candy? Why not.

"Just one more ciggie," she said, "then I'm off."

Less burdened, Dagmar embarked upon a course of light chatter. She sat sucking, slurping, and smoking, and at once everything was wee and twee and impossibly charming. "Oh, it will be lovely to dance at the wedding." Fuck, I thought, not the Tondalaya routine. Is she still doing that? Hair flying all over the place as she dances with abandon, eyes closed, only stopping for a sip and a puff as she slyly counts the house. "And Donald's so looking forward to it. Yes, he's feeling better now. They make such a handsome couple. And I'm painting again. It's going ever so well. You must come to dinner. Oh, you'll take me out to dine? Why I'd love that, really. I know a sweet little place." She was three, her permanent emotional age, and with no Mummy or Daddy she could have all the cake and ice cream she wanted.

When the scales fall from your eyes they drop like hubcaps from a dump truck, crashing and clattering and banging down the highway. It's as if an alarm goes off and you awaken abruptly from a long sleep. Things that were fog-shrouded and hazy from habit become so clear and startling they're seen for exactly what they are. It was not just that her trump, her long suit of beauty, had been played out and would not last the game. The boy — I mean Donald, he is long past being a boy — figures into this. It occurs to me that part of his childhood consisted of being a cattle prod wielded to control me, and now she was missing that tool as well.

When he was a child my access to him was dependant upon my co-operation, my ability to be reasonable, to give in: an ability that was sorely tried, depending on her prevailing mood. I had to change days and times on a whim, be told when to take him in summer and for how long. Basically I had to eat a little shit with every serving. This I did, only losing it once. Then, I pushed her through the bathroom window, not meaning to go so far. "Yah, yah, yah, yah, yah," she was braying with her eyes shut and her hands over her ears so as not to hear what I was saying. Before I could stop myself her ass was hanging out over the back yard and bits of glass were flying everywhere. Got her attention that time. For a while the servings of excrement were larger, but that little bit of mutiny helped the medicine go down.

So I listened and watched while she talked and sipped. She could be very sweet when she wanted something, when she didn't have the power to demand. Because Dagmar, stuck forever in the tantrum phase, rules her narrow world with the iron fist of the despot, benevolent only on occasion, when all the dollies behave. What must it have been like to grow up, like Donald, as one of her dollies? Does he really love his mummy, as he drunkenly professes, or is it a kind of Stockholm syndrome, a hostage embracing their captor in an attempt to survive? He's earned some slack from me because of it. No more, though.

Hearing the shallow monotony of her personal liturgy was getting to me. I could sense the fear. Despair radiated off her in waves. She appeared pathetic, sorrowful. All was not well within the Queendom. She could always turn to Daddy — from whom she never strayed far — until he died. Fucker practically lived forever, ninety-something before he croaked, far too late to help his daughter. We told her — I and the others — that it would come to this. "Yah. Yah. Yah. Yah," she'd say and block her ears. I idly wondered: if I stuck a funnel down her throat and poured in molten lead would she keep talking? How about if she were sawed off at the neck?

"Knock, knock," Ray said, opening the door slowly and poking his head into the room. "May we come in?"

Gandhi pushed past him, not waiting for an answer. Ray followed, squinting to adjust from the glare of the sun. The dog sneezed and Ray, rubbing his eyes with both hands, issued a theatrical cough. His tongue hung out to emphasize the point.

"It certainly is thick in here," he said, blinking rapidly. He spotted the source, Dagmar, a cigarette blazing in her right hand and the mug of coffee she'd been nursing in the other. Her mouth was slightly open and her left cheek, heavy with lozenge, bulged out as she stared at Ray. It was difficult to tell who was more startled, Godzilla or the Wolfman. Ray recovered first.

"Oh, excuse me. I didn't mean to barge."

"Ray, I don't believe you've ever met Dagmar," I said, effecting an introduction. "She's ..."

"I know," he cut me off, "Donald's mummy."

He didn't offer his hand, sensing a possible rebuff. But in the style of the Emperor Ming he pressed his palms together, fingertips to chin, and gave a polite bow.

"Pleezed to meet you."

Dagmar, seldom at a loss for words, croaked out a "charmed, I'm sure," nearly losing her candy in the process.

She would have turned her back on Ray, dismissing him for the scruffy, unimportant person he obviously was, were it not for the dog. Gandhi sat panting from the heat, looking somewhat disheveled. His turban was slightly askew and ringed with dirt. A dark spot had spread over the bump that covered his right ear. Aside from a cursory glance at me, as if to say "Oh yeah, you," Gandhi stared fixedly at Dagmar.

"My, what an interesting dog," she said to no one in particular, then, to Ray, "is it yours?"

"Um, well..." said Ray, putting some thought into it. "So far we're just friends." He paused. "But it looks promising."

"What a funny man you are," Dagmar said, unamused. "What happened there?" she demanded, pointing to Gandhi's head.

"A small incident with a car," I piped in, to Ray's relief. He was not fond of being quizzed. Thing is, with Dagmar, if you let her just ask questions she'll be around to your sex life in no time. How you do it. Probing for areas of discomfort. Going for the kill if she finds any.

"Oh really?" she said, sensing a cover up.

Dagmar snapped the hemline of her dress at Ray — a five — and saw him modestly look down and away. She almost salivated, then shifted on the couch, ready to have a go at him.

"Ouch, fuck!" she hollered, lifting her ass up from the cushion. "Jesus fucking Christ, what is this?" She felt around flat-palmed for the spring that stuck her. I wondered if that might happen. "Fuck, you might have said something, Frank."

"How about: if all our karma be paid back so soon, one could sleep at night though he sin at noon."

"Jesus, what's that supposed to mean?"

"It means it's Weilander's couch," I grinned.

"Bastard," she said. "Fucker." Either at me or Weilander. She rubbed her ass. For sure this was somebody's fault.

Did Gandhi growl or was it just a doggie guffaw? Ray seemed to think it was the latter.

"Be polite, boy," he said, fighting off a smile himself.

"Boy?" Dagmar jeered, rather too loudly. "Well, no wonder it's confused. If she's a boy then where's her little dinky? Or can't you tell the difference?"

Ray's mouth set and Gandhi, not appearing even slightly confused, growled again. Tremolo, more sustained. I would have to explain to Ray later that it was Gandhi's growling, more than the spring-bite, that upset Dagmar. One of her fantasies was that she was Nature Girl, loved by birds and butterflies. Creatures of the forest could fearlessly approach and eat from her hand, a talent her mother apparently had. A dog would never growl at Dagmar.

"Ray, why don't you get Gandhi a drink," I said.

"Good idea," he said, heading for the bathroom.

"Gandhi?" Snorted Dagmar. "Quite the name."

"Ray," I said.

"Yass?"

"There's a plastic container in the kitchen."

"Okaay," he said and changed direction.

The tap came on followed by the deeply satisfying sound of a thirsty dog lapping up water on a hot day. As with many simple acts you could hear the gratitude. Dagmar stubbed her cigarette and defiantly lit another. She knocked back the last of her laced coffee and looked ready to insist on more when Ray poked his furry head back into the room.

"I almost forgot," he said, "one of those policemen is parked up the street."

That gave me pause, but Dagmar went absolutely rigid.

All the anger drained from her face. Her eyes blinked furiously and she looked back and forth at the spot on the couch where she had hidden something, as if rethinking her actions. I immediately sat down beside her, right in the middle of her comfort zone, cutting her off and forcing her to move to the other end of the couch — away from her stash.

"Which cop?" I asked.

"Well, he's not in uniform but it's the big one with the Eskimo name."

"You mean Kuyek?"

"Yass."

"That's Ukranian, not Eskimo," said Dagmar derisively. Ray and I traded a look. "Anyway, that's Roger's partner. How do you guys know him?" She was anxious.

"They dropped in to see Weilander last night, then took him downtown."

"What? You're fucking joking. This is a joke, right?"

I shook my head. It was no joke. While she was distracted I slid my hand between the cushion and the end of the couch. Paydirt. I could feel a plastic-capped pharmacy vial with the tip of my fingers.

"Jesus fucking Christ, talk to me. Is he in jail? Is he there now?"

"Relax, he's at his sister's," I said, reaching for the paper towels and mopping at my face. "Getting hot."

"His sister?" She looked confused.

"Don't you know Weilander's sister?"

"Yes, I fucking know her. Of course I do. She was in the drawing class I gave. Lenore." All indignation now.

I grabbed another square off the roll and dabbed my brow, putting both towels in my pocket. "Waste not, want not," I muttered.

Dagmar, torn between anger and fear, chose the more familiar of the two and exploded.

"Jesus, Frank, you're being an asshole. How did he end up at Lenore's, for fucksakes?"

"Man, what is it with you, Daggie? You seem pretty wound up about this." I saw her calm down a bit, get cagey. "I followed them to the station and got Weilander out of there. Then he drove over to Lenore's. End of story."

"Last night?"

"Last night."

"That fucking asshole." She didn't identify which fucking asshole she was talking about. When you're from the "All men are assholes" school I suppose it doesn't matter.

"Don't worry," I said, getting to my feet. "Weilander told me who the cop was. He wasn't there long enough to say anything. He says he didn't, anyway."

"So you know then?" she said slyly.

"Yes. I know everything."

"Such as?"

"Well, everything," I said vaguely. "All of it."

She laughed. "You don't know a fucking thing do you?"

"Well, what's to know?" I asked, clumsily springing the trap too early, as planned. She bought it.

"Nothing that concerns you, Frankie boy. Anyway I have to go."

She rose from the couch and gathered her things. Somehow her purse fell onto the cushion where I had been sitting. She was about to make a swipe to either retrieve the vial or just ensure it was hidden deep enough. When she manoeuvered her body to hide her actions from me, I spoke again.

"There's one thing I do know, however."

She froze then calmly grabbed her purse and turned to face me.

"What's that?" she asked quietly.

"At least you won't have to introduce me to the boyfriend. We've already met."

I smiled at the flicker of irritation she showed. Then another thought struck her.

"By the way I hope you have lots of this for the wedding," she said, pointing to the roaches she had dumped on the pizza box.

"Tons," I said. "I've got a bunch in the bedroom if you want some."

"No thanks. But hang on to a bit of it at least," she said sweetly.

"Thought you disapproved."

"Well, for a special occasion," she said. And an opportunity to have me busted, I figured.

Turning to Ray in the doorway, talking to him as if he were a child, she asked: "Oh, ah, Ray, is it? Where did you say the policeman was parked?"

"Just above College in the next block. Two cars up."

"Such a lovely day," said Dagmar. "I think I'll walk home by the creek. Where's the back door?"

Gandhi lay on the cool tiles, blocking the way. Ray, seeing Dagmar's step falter, considerately called the dog.

"Here, boy. Let the people out." Gandhi groaned to a standing position and walked over to Ray, taking the long way around the table to avoid Dagmar. It was more of a grumble than a growl we heard as doggie passed by.

"Boy. Ha." Dagmar muttered loud enough for Ray to hear before making her exit. She paused on the back steps.

"We still need to talk," she said. "And soon. How about we go to dinner around seven?"

"Eight would be better for me," I said, knowing how hard it is to drag yourself back from the beach.

"Seven-thirty then," she said and whirled away, not waiting for a reply.

The breeze had stiffened into a real pennant rippler. As I watched her tacking down the alley and up the hill to the bike path, I wondered: Is it just men? Or can women be assholes, too?

The look I got from Ray, as if to say, "What was that?", made me laugh.

"So what do you think of Donald's mummy, Ray?"

"My," he mimicked. "What an interesting Jesus fucking

Christ of a woman."

"Good thing she was on her best behaviour," I said after we stopped laughing.

"Really?"

"Yep. She was after something. It was the dog thing that kept tilting her towards nasty." Then I explained Nature Girl's amazing affinity with animals. How Gandhi's growl threatened her far more than mere physical menace.

"I'm surprised she didn't bring up Satan," I added.

"The Prince of Darkness? I don't think she needs any help from him," concluded Ray.

"Bring up as in mention, not call up, Ray. She had a dog named Satan. Vicious, apparently, except with her. It died last week. Poisoned."

"Oh," said Ray, saddened. "There's been a lot of that lately."

"So Weilander was saying."

"I'd like to see it stopped," said Ray rather firmly. "Just one thing, though."

"What's that, Raymond?"

"Is Satan a boy or a girl?"

"Aw, Ray. Everybody knows that all dogs are boys, just like cats are she's and her's."

"Thank you. That's what I thought, too."

"But you have raised an important theological question, old friend."

"Yass. I have, haven't I?"

"One that requires careful consideration."

"It must be examined thoroughly."

"I just have to make a phone call before we begin."

"And I'm going to look at Gandhi's head."

"Excellent. By the way, Ray, how does the beach sound?"

"Splash. Splash."

"Woof," Gandhi agreed.

chapter nine

While Ray fussed with the dog I pulled the paper towels from my pocket. They were wrapped around the vial Dagmar had hidden in the couch. I had grabbed it the minute I sat down to talk to her. The first towel was used to preserve fingerprints, the second to conceal its bulk. I congratulated myself on the nice bit of legerdemain. Just like riding a bicycle.

The fat amber plastic container with a white cap felt heavier than it should. Using a towel, I pried it open. Inside, a smaller glass vial explained the weight. It was the type used for aromatherapy and held a colourless liquid. The letters GHB were written in marker on the glass. This vial was surrounded by a large number of white, aspirin-sized pills. One side of each was scored so you could snap it in half. The reverse had both the name ROCHE in caps and the numeral 2 with a circle around it.

In the hillbilly backwoods-still days of marijuana I could tell with just one toke whether grass was Mexican, Columbian, Thai, Hawaiian or the newly developed sinsemilla from California. Likewise, from texture and smell, I knew the relative potency and roughly the area of origin of various types of hashish; from blonde Lebanese to the darker Afghani, including an olive-green variety from

India that tasted like rubber and performed about as well. The names, frontier appellations as was befitting pioneers, were exhuberant expressions of folk culture. Panama Red, Acapulco Gold, Purple Queen, Kona Bud, Lady of Light, Thunderfuck, Lambsbreath, Side Road Number Eight.

Two-plus decades later there are far too many varieties to keep track. Thousands of ongoing underground genetic experiments not in the hands of giant pharmaceutical companies — so far as we know — but in the hands of the people, scruffy and bearded though many of them be, have made it impossible to count all the different kinds. This boon of biodiversity is directly due to the prohibition policies of various governments, so a moment of thanks is in order. Skunkweed, the generic term for hydroponic marijuana, stands out for eponymous reasons. But the rest, particularly as it has increased logarithmically in potency, is too diverse to distinguish Ho Chi Minh's Revenge from Clinton's Folly. And yet you can still rely on your nose to give you a pretty decent preview.

What does the number two tell me? Not a fucking thing. Who could ever tell anything by looking at a pill? I've never trusted pills or powders, an attitude so recently enforced by Moyer's "help." You never know what you're getting. Obviously these were pills that were up to something, with intentions that were not honourable. But what? And why did Dagmar stash them at Weilander's?

"What have you got there?" asked Ray, looking up from ministering to the dog.

"Pills," I said, distracted.

"What sort of pills?" Curious Ray.

"I haven't the foggiest, Raymundo."

"Just a minute," he said, "and I'll have a look."

"Will you indeed?" I said. "Well, why not?" Thinking: as if that will help.

Ray finished with Gandhi's new bandage; smaller, cleaner, and with both ears now free. There was a chunk missing from the right one, but aside from a weepy rawness around the edge, it didn't look half bad. I fingered the cut on my cheek, now just a tiny scab.

"Nice job, Ray."

"Thank you."

"Looks more like a yarmulke than a turban now."

"Mm-hmm," said Ray. "Or that little beanie the pope wears. But lets see those pills."

"Just don't touch either vial."

"Okaay," he said and delicately picked up a pill.

"Oh, roofies," he said. "My, my."

"Roofies?"

"Rohypnol," he explained. "You know, date-rape drug. You could stun the senior class of Miss Effie's School for Girls with this much."

"No shit," I said, visualizing a row of plaid-skirted bottoms draped over the paddock fence. Alas, too young and too chubby.

"The rich are getting fatter, Ray." Or I'm getting too old, unable to shape my fantasies.

"Really?"

"Never mind. What about the liquid?" I wondered what Dagmar was doing with this stuff. It wouldn't do for schoolboys — unconscious being their natural state to begin with. Perhaps, as I have long suspected, she has more than a competitive interest in her younger sisters.

"GHB is gamma hydroxybutyrate," said Ray. "The kids call it liquid ecstasy, liquid X. It flushes out of your system quicker than Rohypnol but it can really put you out. Vets use this class of drug as a surgical anesthetic. May I see it?"

"Who are you and what have you done with Ray?" I asked, somewhat surprised by his acumen.

"You-must-do-what-I-say," Ray said in a mechanical space guy voice. "Or-you-will-never-see-your-friend-again." Really getting into it.

"Yeah, yeah," I said, "just don't get your prints on it."

"It should be salty if it's GHB," he said, holding it in the paper towel and unscrewing the lid. He dabbed some on his finger, replaced the cap and tasted it. "Oh yes," he said, "it's sal..." and his voice faded. His eyes fluttered, showing the whites, and his knees began to buckle. He grabbed a corner of the table and swayed, starting to go down.

"Ray. Jesus." I moved to grab him just as he straightened up, grinning.

"Takes about fifteen, twenty minutes to hit," he said.

"Asshole." I laughed. "Anyway how do you know about all this?"

"Well, I try to stay current," was all he offered.

But what he knew was considerable. The 2 on the pill stood for two milligrams. Rohypnol was, generically, flunitrazepam — ten times stronger than valium, which is diazepam — so one roofie equals twenty milligrams of diazepam. Colourless, odourless, and tasteless, it can easily be dropped in a drink. You know the rest. It takes about half an hour to feel the hit, you peak in two hours, and the ride lasts eight to twelve. Among effects such as dizziness and drowsiness, two things stand out. One is that it induces amnesia — a real popular feature with rapists. The other is that, even though it's a sedative, it can provoke aggressive behavior. You can be awake, ambulatory, and violent, and not remember a thing.

What blows me away is that people voluntarily ingest this stuff to enhance the effects of whatever shit they're on — primarily alcohol or cocaine. It's a booster drug, and yet a large dose mixed with alcohol can be lethal. Fascinating, no? As for the GHB, it can kill you outright if you take too much. Whether it's mixed with booze or not.

"So, GHB is stronger than Rohypnol, then," I said to Ray.

"Not really," he said. "They're about the same. It's just harder to judge dosage with a liquid."

"How much do we have here?" Pointing to the glass vial.

"Looks like about twenty milligrams. So times ten it's the equivalent of two hundred mils of diazepam. Lets say enough to send Dumbo and his mummy sleepy-byes for a long time."

"I am amused, Ray, very amused."

"I thought you already knew about this, until you told me about the China White," Ray said.

"Because of Ananah?"

"Yass. She had a low body temperature and a practically non-existent pulse rate."

"C'mon, Ray, how do you come by this sudden expertise?"

"I told you already. I keep informed. That's all. Besides, it's only sudden to you." Ray the Enigma.

"Have it your way." I wouldn't pry any further. For now. There was a stubborn streak under all the grime.

It didn't take a genius to figure out where Dagmar got the pills. Or did it? I shared this with Ray, who shrugged and said nothing. It had to be Shpak, didn't it? But why was she bringing them to Weilander, and did he know? Thinking about it, I was sure that he wasn't aware. Otherwise he would have blurted. Still, he could keep his mouth shut, especially about important stuff, if he was cautioned. And he stayed sober. An icy thought asked: What if they were Weilander's to begin with? Nah.

There were two decisions to make, I thought, as I reassembled the date rape kit. How many roofies to keep for myself, and what to do with the leftovers. I couldn't see needing more than a dozen, so I cut twenty out and put them aside. It looked like a lot. Too much. Okay. I put ten back. Hmm. I remembered the first rule of dispensing drugs from somebody else's stash. Always be generous to yourself, otherwise you'll regret it later.

A slow-motion tennis match ensued, pills going back and forth, finally leaving me with eighteen at set point. Done. No doubt I would regret at some later date not having pills number nineteen and twenty; for the ritual mental mortification of the chronic abuser, if nothing else. Having made one sacrifice the fate of the GHB was easier to decide, particularly in the absence of another glass vial to effect a transfer. I took it all.

"Quite a struggle," noted Ray, who had been watching

the drama unfold with some amusement.

"The only struggle. Dealing with oneself. A pity the Weilander method for distributing dope didn't apply."

"I don't believe I'm familiar with that one."

"It only works when you have a pile of grass and no scale. One guy divides the pile and the other guy gets to pick first. This was just an exercise of greed versus prudence."

"Which reminds me. Should we perhaps fortify ourselves for the trip to the beach?"

"How so?" I asked, the straight man in a never-ending vaudeville routine.

"Well, lets see. Hmm, pizza might be nice."

"Why don't you call now and we'll pick it up on our way out of town," I suggested, not thinking things through.

"Oh, good idea!"

"How much money do you need?" I asked, reaching for my wallet.

"Don't be silly," said Ray, "it's on me."

It very likely will be, I thought. "Didn't you get the ones we had last night?"

"Yass. But it's okay. I have an account."

Ray's credit arrangements were legendary. He avoided the so-called major card companies, or vice versa. However, as a person of substance he had a variety of accounts and minor credit cards from obscure companies and regional chains like Harvey Mart, Western Hardware and Tire, Mel's The Lumber King and Happy Drugs. Whatever he had worked out at Georgie's would be highly prized.

What to do with the rest of the pills became moot. I decided, particularly with Kuyek up the street, that I would take anything incriminating with me until I knew where to stash it. If Dagmar was planning some kind of set-up she was going to be disappointed. All the vial contents, as it were, would come with me, separated into two batches, mine being in a plastic film container. The tons of grass I told Dagmar about was a tad shy of being a quarter ounce. It was coming along for the ride as well, part of it as a joint I would roll for Ray and me. When I thought about it, I went to the coffee table and ate the roaches. Waste not, want not.

Rolling a joint in the bedroom I decided to take all my stuff from Weilander's. It was only one carry-on anyway. This would make me mobile and harder to pin down. Something was circling. I could feel it. I packed and took everything out to the car. Ray was still on the phone, schmoozing and making pizza arrangements. I used my cell phone to call Robbie.

"It's good you called, Frank," said Robbie after we had exchanged pleasantries.

"I almost didn't."

"Figured you wouldn't. Glad I'm wrong."

"So, what's your day like?" I asked.

"I'm free until eight, then I gotta go to the shop."

"How come you're still doing nights, Robbie? You should be wearing the white shirt by now. Superintendent at least."

"Buckskin ceiling," he laughed. "Besides, they call me 'Chief' anyway. Just not to my face."

"Go figure," I said, and then outlined my plans for the beach. Robbie said he needed to stay closer to town so we settled on Christophe's, a semi-private beach just past the town of Craven. It was owned by a farm family who didn't seem to mind people using it. We were to meet there at four. I rounded up Ray and Gandhi.

"Here's my idea for a seating plan, Ray," I said, remembering in time there would be food in the car. "You two sit in back. That way it will be easier to share the pizza with ... ah ... him. I just want one slice anyway."

"Okaay," he said, "good idea. And since you're just having a bit we can eat one pizza now and save the other for a late afternoon snack."

"Whatever." Of course he would order two. What was I

thinking? I asked Ray if he wanted a towel and he informed me, very firmly, that he would not be swimming, thank you.

"Who's talking about swimming?" I asked.

"Ha ha," he said, after a brief time delay.

I asked Ray to keep an eye on the fat shadow when we drove by.

"He's sleeping," said Ray, as we slowly passed Kuyek in his ghost car.

On the second pass around the block I looked right at him. Fat Boy's head was slumped back at an angle, resting against the door pillar. Definitely in dreamland.

"Too bad, in a way," I said as we headed for Georgie's.

"Why's that?"

"We're not going to know if he was waiting for us or Weilander."

"Or somebody else."

"Or somebody else. Say, Ray, you're really paying attention to all this shit."

"More than you think," he said. "Besides, it's fun."

From the outskirts of the city, where Pasqua Street intersects with Highway 11, it only takes about a half hour to drive to Christophe's. Add ten to fifteen minutes if you turn off the divided highway and meander along the gravelled back roads on the rim of the valley to Craven, from which it's another few miles on two-lane blacktop. When travelling with free-spirited souls such as Ray and Gandhi you may need more time. For them it is definitely the journey, not the destination. Slightly over two hours ought to do it nicely.

Gandhi was well on the mend as evidenced by his interest in the slice of pizza Ray tried to hand me from the back seat.

"Try to get me one without drool or a nose print on it, okay? And keep the dog off it, too."

"Ha ha," said Ray. "I'm trying, but doggie loves his 'za."

So the first slice went to Gandhi, Ray holding it for both bites. He held the next wedge in the air to pass to the front seat, but with the dog licking Ray's face just as we hit a dip in the road, it ended up sticking to the ceiling. Slice two for doggie, minus the tomato sauce and mushroom bits plastered on the fabric above Ray's head.

"Whoopsy," said Ray as the third portion fell to the back seat prior to being scorfed by our canine friend. "This isn't working out so good, except for you-know-who."

So off-road, down a dusty grid, we had a picnic beside a derelict wooden grain bin that had once been red. It sat at the corner of a field lying fallow. Everything that resembled pizza was relentlessly sought out and consumed by the pair of ravenous beasts. I was allotted one smallish wedge that, prudently, I ate rather quickly.

"What happened to saving one for later?" I asked idly, still sitting in the car.

"Well," explained Ray, "Gandhi isn't all that comfortable dealing with the abstract. Are you, boy? Noo. It's all here and now with him."

"Good of you to help out," I said.

"Yass," agreed a contented Ray. "Well, too much tomato sauce will give him gas. I know it gives me gas."

"Oh no," I said, recognizing the danger. "How much time do we have?"

"None!" laughed a maniacal Ray as he let loose a lazy, lingering, unsuppressed pronouncement of gaseous braggadocio that propelled me instantly from the front seat.

I sat on the grass in the shade of the car upwind of Castor and Pollux, the Dioscuri of methane, who were exchanging vaporous editorials on the substance of their lunch. It was not for nothing the Romans worshipped this pair before going into battle. In a short while the volleys subsided in frequency and intensity. To be completely accurate, it was Ray making all the noise. Gandhi's efforts, though no less lethal, were barely audible.

"Would now," I posed aloud, "be a better time to toke up than waiting for the beach?" One hearty concurrence plus one abstention — or silent assent, one could not be sure —

and the motion was carried.

Half a joint later I tuned in to the big show that's going on all around us but too seldom notice. Of course the reception is always better out of cities, away from traffic, telephones, people with titles and the grooves that guide us to our daily duties. Here the wind is tangible as it moves along: sighing, puffing, gusting, and playing dead, pretty much as it always has done.

A red-tailed hawk, perched motionless on a fence post, has her feathers teased as she waits patiently for dinner. That same air rises in visible support of her mate, who wheels in slow circles high above the neighboring field. The leaves of the poplar, under which Robbie said the elders preferred to sit on the hottest days, shimmied and sighed, directing the breeze downward to the base of the trunk. The topmost leaf, already a brilliant yellow, fluttered against the blue backdrop of the sky like a Chinese postage stamp on an airmail envelope. A small tumbleweed skitters by; veering left, then stopping, veering right, then stopping. It suddenly lurches onward, reeling and skipping rootlessly down the dusty road like a drunken pilgrim.

Poole believed that civilization is a passing fancy — like the hula hoop. I think perhaps he's right. Certainly the fence posts, the highway over there, the roads, the houses, and the fields — especially the fields — are never more than a season or two from being reclaimed entirely. Meanwhile, whether we pack up our tents and go or not, it's pretty much business as usual to those who have not severed their covenant with the land. Deer sleep lightly in the islands of trees that dot the seas of wheat and barley. The bees are still working the bobbing landing pads of roadside flowers.

"Noo, doggie. Like this. Slurp slurp. See."

Ray is in the back seat trying to get Gandhi to lick the tomato sauce off the ceiling. Like all great educators he is teaching by example. Failing that, however, he turns to the stain on the seat. All Gandhi will do is lick the bits off Ray's beard when their faces are in proximity.

"Nice technique, Ray. And please convey my thanks to doggie for getting you to clean up so nicely."

"Convey them yourself," said Ray in exasperation. It was time to move on.

There was a newish half-ton at Christophe's, up on the side of the hill where people park. I took it to be Robbie's since he was the only person I could see. I wondered what he would make of my companions. Gandhi stopped briefly, looked at Robbie, looked at Ray, and then led us down to the beach. The dog sniffed at Robbie, who ignored him, looking instead at Ray. I was going to introduce them when Robbie spoke.

"Hello, Ray. Frank didn't tell me he was keeping such good company today."

"Robbie," said Ray, making his Emperor Ming bow.

Robbie would have none of that and strode over to give Ray a big hug which quickly turned into a back-slapping session.

"Almost time for a bath, huh?"

"It's getting close," said Ray, shivering in mock fear.

"So, you still playing the fool, Ray?"

"As long as I can get away with it."

chapter ten

In baseball it's where the team sits between innings; in the jungle it's a canoe. On the prairie it's a man-made hole in the ground, of various depths and sizes, designed to collect and hold water. The dugout is cousin to the slough, which is more or less its natural version. And sloughs are ambitious puddles — loaded with aquatic plants — whose collective total on the prairie alone supports over two-thirds of the entire duck population of North America.

If you took one of these puddles and stretched it out from north to south for sixty miles, and made it a couple of miles across at its widest point, you would have Last Mountain Lake, no doubt so named because the last thing you would expect to see around here would be a mountain. A lot of people just call it Long Lake. On the east and west shores the various beaches that dot the southern end of the lake are the heart of cottage country. At first I refused to swim here, loving water as I do. I got over it. Yes, it was muddy looking and, true, you had to wade through a few feet of green slime to get there. But it was fresh water, untreated, and untouched by industrial waste. Unlike, say, the toxic soup of lakes Ontario and Erie. Run-off from agricultural chemicals and pesticides contributed to the excessive algae growth making it less than pristine, but to someone who had spent the entire summer swimless in Toronto, it was deluxe.

I was all thrash, splash and float, diamonds sparkling in my eyes. Standing submerged up to my neck, I watched Ray and Robbie talking and laughing like old friends. Gandhi inspected the beach with his nose, following invisible trails. To hell with them, I thought. I'm not going to ask how it is they know one another. But I better see what Robbie wants.

"You have to watch it with this guy, Frank. I'm telling you. He's mean, sneaky and not stupid. He shouldn't be on the force." Robbie was warning me about Shpak. "He knows that, which makes him very dangerous."

"So how is it he does have a badge and gun?" I asked, toweling off.

"I don't know. The tests weren't as good when he joined, maybe. They'd catch him now, I think. Could be the job changed him. In the twenty years he's been working he mighta got twisted up. Usually guys like him quit or get the boot. Shpak is different. He likes being the way he is, and so far he's too smart to get caught."

"Okay, I hear you. I'll stay away from the bastard. Except with all this wedding shit and me supposed to have dinner with Dagmar, I don't see how to avoid him."

"Could be too late, anyway," Robbie said ominously.

"Whaddya mean?"

"If he's onto you he might not let go."

"Isn't that swell."

"He's a crazy bastard, Frankie. Not crazy like you, crazy in a deliberate, destructive way."

"Crazy like me? What's that supposed to mean?"

"What do I mean, Ray?"

"You mean when he gets exasperated, acts precipitously, and doesn't care about the consequences?"

"That'll do," Robbie grinned.

"Thank you both." I blew an Italian kiss with my hand.

"You're welcome," came their response, in unison.

Though they were just kidding around, I do have a bit of a temper. Or, rather, used to. It's pretty much under control now. Nothing like the permanent state of rage that seems to be invested in Donald.

"Frank, you're an 'in your head' kinda guy. Who knows what you got going on in there? Always working on something. Schemes, theories ... whatever. But you care about people and don't mean anybody any harm. Most of the time, anyway," he added, catching a flash in my eyes.

"Mmm-hmmm," amenned Ray, softening things.

"Shpak doesn't care. And I'm telling you this because he can hurt you. He will hurt you if he gets a chance."

"Okay, Robbie. Take it easy. I only just met the guy. In fact, I didn't even meet him, just his fat friend, Kuyek."

"Kuyek," snorted Robbie. "He's just Shpak's toady. Really dumb. But watch him, too, because he does whatever he's told."

"Seems fair enough, eh, Ray?"

"Specially since he's watching us," said Ray.

We told Robbie about Kuyek's stakeout on Weilander's place. He laughed when we mentioned Fat Boy napping, saying that it was par for the course. Then he stopped and looked away for a bit, thinking hard about something.

A large shadow passed over us, then another, slowly sliding along the sand. A pair of enormous white pelicans with eight-foot wingspans were practically motionless as they sailed by. They were so low you could count their black wing feathers. A true prairie bird, they nest here and winter south, like some farmers whose pesticides are killing them for the privilege of doing the same. And also, like the true prairie, they are vanishing. Aiding and abetting the insecticides are the idiots who shoot them, looking for the snow geese that are half their size. Then there's the well-meaning eco-types that scare adults off their nests long enough for the chicks to fry in the sun.

"Fewer every year," said Robbie, who then mumbled something in Plains Cree. A benediction.

Ray was open-mouthed and wide-eyed. "They're beautiful," he said. "This is the first time I've ever seen one. And so close!"

"Another argument for the termination of the species," I said, voicing my thoughts aloud.

"What?" said Ray, incredulously.

"Not them, Ray. Us."

"Oh," he said, mollified. "I can live with that."

"So how buzzed are you guys, anyway?" Robbie asked.

"What are you, a cop?" I snapped. For some reason the question made me wary.

"Always the smart answer, Frankie. What you should be asking is who I am, not what I am. Like you do with Ray here."

"Easy, Rob. Getting a bit serious, aren't you?"

"That's the idea."

"It's okay. I get it. Shpak's a bad guy. Watch myself. Okay, I'm watching. And thank you."

Robbie stared at me for a minute. His eyes were focussed and far away at the same time. He looked at Ray, who nodded as if something had passed between them. Then he looked up and watched the pelicans rhythmically doing three wingbeats and a rest stroke to the other side of the lake. Whump-whump-whump, glide. Whump-whump-whump, glide. Pretty much as they always have done. Then Robbie spoke.

"When I became a cop I had what I thought were good reasons. It was sad to see my friends distance themselves. Especially you, Frank. But at least you showed your anger; were up front about it. Ray was the only one who didn't change. The rest? Well, it was lonesome for a while. Since most of the arrests we make around here are of First Nations people, I at least have contact with my brothers and sisters. I make sure they're treated right, and try to help whether they curse me or not. In a few years I'm retired, and it can't come soon enough. Socially I'm an outcast, but in the course of my work, on the beat or behind the desk, I think more people have been happy to see me than not. If I can still say that on my last day, it will be enough. As for you, Frank, I hope it isn't you who have forgotten who your friends are." He looked me straight in the eye and added with a grin, "Despite you and Brenda in the teepee."

The look on my face caused Robbie and Ray to laugh. Red-faced, I joined in.

"That was some snore then, from a guy who was really awake," I said to Robbie.

"Yeah. I even made it irregular. Like you would, Frankie, you tricky bastard."

"She wasn't for you, Robbie. What can I say? I'm surprised you didn't have a go at Dagmar to get even."

"Who says I didn't?" he said, booming out a laugh.

When a person smokes too much pot they fall asleep for a while. They don't get into a car and drive on the wrong side of the road into a school bus. They don't go home and slap their family around. They don't get into fights in bars. They don't try to fill an inside straight with the rent money. They don't get all teary and beery and mournfully lament what might have been. The alteration of consciousness is a normal pursuit for humans and other mammals. However, those who prefer this from a plant that grows anywhere, to the elixirs produced from complex distilling processes, are labeled criminals. Those who prefer enlightenment to enfeeblement are hunted and prosecuted. Those who shrug and say "To each his own" are rounded up and roped by the forces of people who say "This is the only way." That's why I got pissed off when Robbie became a cop. He was joining the enemy. And he knew it.

Now that I realize that it is fear and alcohol dependence that blinds society — and that the weaning process is going to take a while longer — I no longer see it as a black-and-white issue. Besides, Robbie had an entirely different agenda, with far less selfish motives. I knew that.

"Truce," I said, holding up my palm.

"Truce. We got some laughing to catch up on, Frank. But not just yet. Take care of business first."

"So you don't want a toke then?" I asked.

"Not before work. Ask me on the weekend."

"I will."

"First," he said, "let's get this little item out of the way. You got a certain judge on your list that you think is cool. You're wrong. They're going to nail you."

There it goes again, that roaring in my ears. Robbie really threw me. How does he even know about my subscription list, never mind who's on it?

Once a year I go cross-country, from Toronto to Vancouver, visiting subscribers. They pay a fee, substantially below market for quantity, and a few weeks later receive a pound of the finest quality herb from a grower's collective on the west coast. It's a pleasant and lucrative hobby. I don't handle the stuff. I just take the orders and collect the money — from which I deduct "the fair profit of able dealing," as Lao Tzu would say.

It's a small list. Everyone on it is adult, and well-known to me. Or they come recommended from someone I trust completely. I knew the judge personally, very personally, before she became a judge. And that was the real shocker. I would not have thought she would ever turn on me. She was one of the original subscribers. Since long before she took the bench.

"Say something, Frank," said Robbie.

"How about 'gulp,'" I said, literally stunned. "I mean, how do you know this, Robbie? Is it common knowledge down at the station?"

"I can't tell you everything right now," he said. "But no, it isn't common knowledge. I got lucky, Frank, which means you got lucky. If you handle it right."

"You have my full attention. Fuck. This blows me away."

Ray, bored or sensing heaviness, had gone walking with Gandhi. The dog patrolled the shoreline while Ray stayed up on the beach, well away from the water.

"Ray doesn't know anything about this," I said.

"He wouldn't say anything even if he did," said Robbie. "This has got nothing to do with Ray. Hell, Frank, it isn't even all about you. You're just a little action on the side in this game."

"How am I supposed to react to that?"

"Just listen," he said. "What do you think of someone who drugs people and takes advantage of them when they're under?"

Now there's a question. A number of thoughts and answers sprang to the fore, champing at the bit, tearing down the track, competing.

"Frank?"

"Huh?"

"You still with us?"

"Sorry, Robbie, my mind was racing."

"Oh."

"Well, assuming you're talking about a male, I think we should nail his balls to a stump and push him over backwards."

"Good plan. But what if the person was female?"

"Take the long way home and avoid conflict at all costs?"

"Really," he said, shaking his head from side to side. "And if it's a cop?"

"Aha," I sighed. "Oh yes. Now some things are making sense. Thank you, Robbie, and I just might have a gift for you."

"Okay."

"Shpak," I spat. "He's the guy."

"All I need is proof." He paused. "By the way, if anyone asks ..."

"We didn't have this conversation," I finished. "Same goes for me, Rob. Especially with what I'm going to tell you. So everything is a 'what if' — supposing, not declaring. You don't have to act on 'what ifs'."

"Agreed."

Ray rejoined us. "What did I miss?" he asked.

"Everything," I said.

"Not much," said Robbie.

"Thank goodness," said Ray. "Carry on as if I weren't here." Then he flopped onto the sand, silently amused about something.

When I finished telling Robbie about Dagmar's visit and deposit in the couch bank, he threw his head back and laughed. Every now and then I am reminded how large Robbie is physically. This was one of those times.

"She's some piece of work," he said.

"She scares the hell out of me," I said.

"Me too."

"That makes it unanimous, then," added Ray.

"So you figure these pills are roofies?" asked Robbie.

"That's what Ray says. I've never even heard the term before."

"That right, Ray?"

"Yass. And the liquid is probably GHB."

"Good enough for me," said Robbie, not questioning Ray's assessment at all. "But what liquid? You didn't mention any liquid, Frank," said Robbie, turning all cop for a minute.

"Oh yeah. There was a small glass vial in with the pills with a bit of clear liquid in it," I said offhandedly, as if I had inadvertently omitted that detail. Bigmouth Ray. Robbie stared thoughtfully at me.

"That's an important detail, Frank. Very important. You have to tell me everything if this is going to work." Looking right at me.

"Of course," I agreed. "So, did I tell you that if there were any prints on the container they would still be there?" I explained about the paper towels.

"Where are the vials now?"

"Close."

"How close?"

"Close enough, Robbie. Now you talk."

"I have to have them, Frank."

"And so you shall," I promised. "But how are you going to explain how you got them?"

"Let's check for prints first and worry about that later."

"What if mine show up somehow?"

"We'll deal with that if we have to."

"How?"

"I don't know. Look, Frank, the worst-case scenario here is that you'll have to testify that you found the pills and handed them in to me."

"Then what, I get all the cheese I want?"

"You're no rat, Frank, think about what's happening. It won't come to that anyway."

"Hmmm."

"Listen. About a year ago we took down a couple of guys at the Wander Inn on Vic East. They were a travelling pharmacy. Part of the haul was a shitload of roofies and GHB. Shpak and Kuyek made the bust. They nailed two guys, although we thought there was supposed to be a third. One of the bad guys kept an inventory list and there appeared to be a serious discrepancy in the roofie department, but everything else tallied up pretty good. Shpak must have missed that; or, more likely, Kuyek. Even so, nobody made much of it. I picked up on it right away, and so did another guy who also wants to nail Shpak and any other cop who isn't right. We decided to wait and see what happened.

"For a long time it was business as usual. Then the rumours started. Women, mostly in and around the arts community, would wake up, sometimes in strange places, sore in the vaginal area, unable to remember anything about the night before. Some of them were so freaked out, they sought psychiatric help. We caught a couple of kids working 'Pub Nite' at the university, but couldn't make a connection. In the meantime, the evidence for our original felons somehow gets misnumbered, and by the time that's cleared up, these guys are out and long gone. Guess who allowed bail and set a ridiculously low figure?"

"Trudy?"

"'Fraid so, Frank. Judge Jackson herself."

"Fuck. She really wanted to be a judge. I didn't think this bad. Somebody must have caught her toking up."

"Worse than that. She's part of that arts crowd now."

"Shit, yeah, that's pretty bad all right," I said, getting a laugh out of both of them.

"I think she's one of the victims," said Robbie, being serious again. "And, if the rumours are true, whoever is behind this activity is taking pictures."

"She might enjoy that," I said. "At least under other circumstances. I'd be more worried about that meticulous diary she keeps if I were her."

"Now you're there," Robbie said.

"Jesus, Robbie. If Shpak gets hold of that diary it isn't just Trudy that's fucked."

"He had it, but he got careless. Now he doesn't."

"You have it?"

"Not me, but it's safe. They all are. There's five of them."

"Christ no," I thought out loud. Friend or no, I had to get those diaries from Robbie. I remember trying to get them from Trudy, but she had hidden them too well.

"That's right, Frank, you devil. You're a big feature in the first one. Lotta mentions in the others, too. You left kinda sudden, huh?" He was kidding around, maybe even trying to make me feel better, but I was squirming.

"It was never that serious. Besides, you know how much I'd like to be Mr. Judge."

"Reads like she was pretty serious."

"You can't believe everything you read. Fuck, you should know that." I said, trying not to let too much irritation show. "So, she's working with Shpak to set me up. That bitch! Jesus, are there any women you can trust?"

"People, Frank, not women. And the answer is no, not when they're trying to save their own ass. This I have learned."

"And what about Dagmar? She's bringing shit over to stash at Weilander's. Is it a set-up? Is she in on all this?"

"That's what I can't figure. We need to think about that."

"Robbie, your truck is ringing," said Ray. Gandhi must have told him. I still couldn't hear it.

"Be right back," said Robbie. He ran up the hill gracefully, light on his feet, no gut. The guy was in great shape.

It was dumb, that bit about the trustworthiness of women. They aren't any less — or more — trustworthy than men. They aren't even 'they' in the true cosmic sense. I know all that. A stupid hoser remark, something you say in a sports bar.

They've got interesting brains, though, if we are to believe the latest research. Efficient, multi-tasking units that never shut down. Running all the time. Men's focus on the main chance, occasionally juggling gum-chewing with walking, before going semi-dormant to recharge. When this study on male and female brains was published, replete with chromatographical evidence indicating hot spots, my boyhood pal Randall phoned. "See," he said, "I told you they never sleep." His lifelong thesis.

When you just can't figure something out it becomes easier to rely upon solutions provided by other people. Trusted people who have proven their mettle in other ways. Bad idea. But I've done that from time to time. Tried stuff out. When Larry Wright, who I looked up to when I was twelve and he was thirteen, said studying music was for saps, I turned down guitar lessons from my uncle. It hadn't occurred to me that Larry was lousy at music. Seeing a kid with a guitar case at a bus stop, I passed Larry's wisdom on. "It's for saps, you know."

"Sez who?"

"I'm just sayin'."

He looked at me warily, as if I had escaped from somewhere, and got on his bus. I felt really, really stupid.

Larry could scrap, though. There was no fear of the ferocious and numerous red-haired Chisholms when he was around. Like Randall, Larry provided me with all kinds of information about girls. Randall at least had sisters. Unlike Larry or I. But over time, and into adulthood, he's proven only slightly more reliable on matters regarding the distaff side than your average sheet of plywood. I became better informed, Randall's sisters bedamned, because of cousin Vicki.

There was no love lost between Vicki and me. Same age, each the eldest child, we lived next door to one another, her mother and mine being sisters. In context, the research indicating that intelligence is passed on primarily from the mother's side, proves credible. Vicki would sit on top of the wooden swing and taunt me if she got a better mark at the multi-grade country school we attended. I was as clever, but not nearly as good a taunter when our positions reversed, as they frequently did. For one thing, she'd cover her ears and stick her tongue out whenever I was crowing. Had not the Everlasting fix'd His canon 'gainst punching girls, I would have slugged her many times over.

She showed me hers and I showed her mine under Grampy's cottage in the way six-year olds eternally shall. As soon as our clothes were back on she denied it ever happened, and has stuck to that story ever since. Fine. A year or two later we played hostage at her suggestion. She was to be the hostage. I tied her hands behind her back. Lie on your belly, I told her. I tied her ankles. Then, by mutual consent, I gagged her. The next innovation, mine, came from a comic book, The Lone Ranger. I tied another rope to the one at her ankles and bent her knees straight up until her feet pointed at the ceiling. Then, not allowing any slack, I tied the other end around her neck. She lay face down and helpless, her stomach the base of an isosceles triangle, hog-tied. Now she was a hostage! It was a fine job. The masked man would be proud. Of course, every time she moved her legs she would choke. That was the whole idea.

Vicki panicked and started gagging, thrashing around, strangling herself. As I attempted to loosen the knots, being no less terrified myself, she would kick them tighter. By then she was turning purple. Enter her father. My uncle, by marriage not blood. He cut the rope with a butcher knife to save her life.

My cousins were not allowed to play with me after that. An edict, I realize, that has yet to be rescinded.

Like I cared. It was a relief, more than anything. My uncle said some things I no longer remember, although I detested him to the day he died. Vicki cried forever, even snuffling while she ate her ice cream. I stayed in the corner, awaiting my mother. When the adults looked away she'd stare at me sideways with a wicked, gloating grin. I wished for her to become fat.

Robbie looked grim striding back to the beach. He looked at me.

"Gotta go," he said.

"What's up?"

"Do you know Jane Kramer?"

"Janey," said Ray.

"I've heard of her," I said.

"She's been found dead. We don't know why yet. No obvious signs."

"This would be the same Janey that Weilander saw Shpak with a couple of nights ago."

"That right?" Robbie said, his eyes hardening. "I better find Weilander, then, before Shpak does."

"This is terrible," said Ray. "She was very sweet."

"Bring me that stuff, Frank. Quick!"

"Can you meet me around seven thirty?" I asked.

"Will you have the roofies?"

"Yes. How about the 13th Avenue Safeway lot?"

"I'll be there. Wait if I'm a few minutes late," he said, before making his exit and telling Ray to watch out for me.

As if, I thought.

"Why didn't you just give them to him now?" asked Ray, as he waved bye-bye.

"I would have, Ray, except there's one little thing I have to do first. And I don't mean this last swim." Then I took a running flat dive into the cool brown water.

After all, I had a dinner date.

chapter eleven

On sober second thought, Trudy would be the most likely candidate to betray me. She had more to lose than anyone on my list. And, since she was never long on sentiment, she wouldn't let feelings get in the way. Trudy was for Trudy. If a gun were pointed at my head she'd be the first one I'd betray, too. So, in a way, that made it fair. She didn't even smoke dope for cosmic or recreational reasons. Trudy was one of the migraine people. As well, she had chronic, low-level back pain. Interested in marijuana primarily for its analgesic qualities, enlightening thoughts or flashes of humour were side effects she endured. Trudy was a rather serious girl — with one interesting exception.

Barefoot, she stood five-ten-and-a-half. Quite a package, when I first knew her in the biblical sense. She was a slightly undernourished mesomorph, more than willowy, less than full, with shoulder-length blonde hair. Bee-stung lips, gorgeous teeth. Breasts that were, if anything, a bit too large. And somewhere behind the coke-bottle lenses of unwieldy, chunky glasses was a pair of pale blue eyes. Contacts didn't work for Trudy — they hurt, and were used sparingly to help correct the extreme myopia which, unfortunately, also extended to her view of life. Literally and figuratively, Trudy could not see past the end of her nose.

Part of her charm was that you could have some fun with that.

Much as she disliked this particular diminution of her name, she loved it when I'd say, "Nobody is equal to you, Trude." Driven as she was by deficiency motivation she couldn't get enough of it. But what I meant was there were only two kinds of people for Trudy, those who were better than she and those found wanting. So, she was either sucking up to someone or lording it over them and forever worried about where she stood. I hear she is a pretty good arbiter of justice in which I suspect this desire of hers to be correct in all things plays a major role. Plus, in some measure of the karmic balance of the sexes, cute, rough-around-the-edges guys would always fare better than expected in her courtroom. Why is what made Trudy great.

Trudy had a voracious appetite for sex. In public she would walk around like she had a carrot stuck up her ass. She lived in terror that she or her companion du jour would commit some indelible gaucherie, thereby suffering great embarrassment. Privately, the terror might well be reversed, and there's no telling where that carrot could end up. Her approach to sex was so boldly selfish, so geared to pleasing Trudy, so unapologetically this-is-for-me-ish that it was an absolute turn on. It was every man for himself — after she was finished, of course. And it was an attitude, a feeling, more than the sum total of her actions, which might have provided a large measure of emotional content in different circumstances. At least she did most of the work and you didn't have to worry about pleasing her. Trudy pleased herself. You were merely an instrument — like Gabriel's trumpet or da Vinci's brush.

The candle was lighted. The heavy glasses that stayed on so she could peer at you while you undressed were placed with a thunk on the night table. And, as was typical, they'd fall, being only half placed, clattering to the floor. The single sheet would slip off as the rising full moon with its curved exclamation point would sway and rove the firmament while she groped in vain for vision. Abandoning her search, she would turn and smile vaguely in your direction, and lie back, arms at her side, flat, deceptively rigid, seemingly unapproachable. The sheet, draped across her stomach, would be artfully arranged under her navel, exposing the dark tree line that led south to a thicker forest whose contours could be seen bulging beneath the soft cotton cover.

You would be forgiven for thinking this must be Sunday School Girl's first real date. Except her lips were slightly parted, moist. And her teeth were not clenched at all but lay there fat and white in two glistening reefs through which swirled the rapid ebb and flow of her shallow breathing.

Nostrils, as those of a thoroughbred, were slightly flared and quivering. Her eyelashes fluttered. And in reaching to sort an errant lock of hair it would always be a little thrilling to casually brush her nipple with your wrist and see it pop to attention like an airbag on a limousine.

To touch her now, somewhere, anywhere — a toe, her shoulder, the base of her neck — would elicit a soft gasp and a keening moan, like the plaintive call of a Celtic harp. It is merely the vibration from the centre of the web; the sound of metaphors clashing, just as you are thinking: Shit, man, this is easy.

The next moment would be the nanosecond of awe that lives in brief half-life after the flash of lightning and before the thunderclap. A flood of urgent wet kisses would drive you onto your back and race in a torrent to envelop a phallus by now so erect the skin was strained and tightened like a bratwurst splitting on the grill. Sliding up and down and moaning with her mouth locked on like a greased lamprey, she would drive herself madder with each suck, uttering cries that approached melancholy, groans that mimed despair. Her mouth would slip off a cock so stiff it would slap against your stomach in the universal distress call of the beaver. Then down she would dive again, blundering blindly towards the target. No fear, she could find you in the blackest night like the pick of the litter on the fullest teat. What matter a poked eye here, a dented cheek there?

When she could stand it no longer, when she was driven to the absolute limit, she would rise to her knees and straddle your chest like a golden-limbed colossus raining sweet drops of warm nectar. Collapsing on your stomach like a wet sponge, she would leave a scented trail as she slid bump by bump down your abs and onto your member like a hot pot of oiled wax onto a greased pole. The chute is open and the bronco bucks wildly as she rides screaming, her back arched, both arms behind her, in a drunken fury until in a sorrowful wail of profanity she, O Jesus!, explo-oh-oh-oh-odes in giant spasms that fade to a soft mewing as each throbbing beat of death quietly ebbs away. After the first time you might lie there, with an ache; stiff as the handle on Weilander's fridge door, and too astonished to come.

"You'd think two lanes would be enough. Wouldn't you boy?" said Ray, rubbing Gandhi's turban as my tires hit the gravel shoulder.

"Shit! Sorry," I said, straightening the wheel. Maybe I should concentrate more on what to do about Trudy now than what had gone on before — or come off, as the case may be.

Trudy was never that difficult to handle as long as you made it look like she was winning. She fancies herself quite complex, a notion I always encouraged. Never once did she so much as guess I had a black belt in the kind of emotional judo she employed. Trudy reasons, on a level hidden to her, that anybody who could be interested in her must somehow be deficient and therefore unworthy. The sad part here being she's so fucked up she's right. And there is no cure. I ought to know, I practically wrote the manual on that one.

There's a point at which all that sucking up outweighs the sucking. You can be shushed once too often while some third-rate asshole pontificates. Add that to my somewhat hypocritical distaste — since I wear them days on end — at discovering that she was the only woman I ever met that didn't change her underwear at least once a day. That, and the toast crumbs on a chin that would eventually triple in size — along with the rest of her, signalled the end of my private rides on the human tilt-a-whirl. Now it seems the Trude may have been more miffed than I realized.

But should we go for all-out war? Let it percolate for a bit.

Ray and Gandhi were more or less quiet in the back. All four windows were still open. The wind rushed past me, which was the idea. Nevertheless, the odd powerful cross gust intimated of odours produced in the back seat that would be quite satisfactory to their authors but no one else.

"So, Ray," I began in the spirit of scientific inquiry, "how long could one wear undershorts comfortably before needing a change?"

"Do you mean hours in a day or day after day?" he responded, taking the science part seriously.

"Day after day."

"Well, I don't keep records but I've had this pair since the beginning of June." He paused, thinking. "I guess there's a few more good weeks in them. Then I'll have to buy more."

"You mean you buy them one pair at a time?"

"Heavens, no. I get the twin packs at Harvey Mart. Couple of those does me quite nicely for the year."

"You don't launder?" I continued, somewhat fascinated.

"Well, I'm a bit fussy," he admitted, almost embarrassed. "I like a fresh change. Besides if you knew how much fecal matter is passed on in those commercial machines ..."

"I see." Letting that one slide. Pressing on. "What about if you were female?"

"Hmmm. Yaass. I think about that too, sometimes," he said dreamily.

"No, Ray. In terms of underwear change."

"Whoops. Ha ha." He seemed disappointed at being stopped there. "Well, the vagina is kind of a friendly environment ..."

"You don't know Dagmar."

"Very funny. Anyway, a friendly environment for little greeblies and stuff. So I'd say, oh, six, seven days max."

"Thanks, Ray," I said, privately resting my case.

"No problem," said Ray, not expressing any further curiosity on the matter. As we approached the city I asked Ray where I should let him off.

"Aren't you going back to Weilander's?"

"I have a bunch of running around to do before I meet Robbie. Then it's dinner with Dagmar. Besides, Ray, I'm not even sure I'm going to spend any more time at Weilander's. It's getting kinda busy around there."

"Well, you're certainly welcome to stay with me. But we'll have to wait until after dark."

"Thanks, Ray." Thinking that it would be way down my list of places to stay. "Why after dark? Not ashamed of me are you?"

"I'd be proud to have you," he said, making me a little ashamed of myself. "It's just that there are no dogs allowed in my building so I'll have to smuggle Gandhi in later. At least he isn't a barker. Are you, boy?" He thumped the dog's ribs.

"Woof. Woof," concurred Gandhi.

"All right, come on my rounds with me and then we'll go to Weilander's." I was thinking that he should be home by now. Maybe Ray could stay there for a few days.

First, the liquor store. I picked up a bottle of wine and a mickey of Scotch. Then, on to a small building in the industrial district where I rented a sizeable storage locker. Even though I've been gone for years a lot of my stuff has stayed behind; treasures mostly, like my vinyl LPs, eggshell porcelain from China, camping gear, old clothes, and my model 870 Remington Wingmaster twelve-gauge pump.

I could even crash here in a pinch, I realized as I let myself in and walked down the dusty corridor lit by a bank of metal-shaded lights. My twelve-by-eighteen-foot space was a third full, if that. Who would know? I don't think I've ever seen anyone else in here, despite the fact that there were maybe ten other lockers. The office that never failed to debit my credit card every month was on the next block in a more modern building. I tried the taps in the small washroom I passed. Not only a sink but hot water, too, after letting it run for a bit. The toilet worked. The building was heated and from previous, somewhat paranoid, expeditions I knew there was a trap door off a catwalk that led to the roof next door and down into an alley.

With a key that otherwise sits useless on a ring for fifty-one weeks a year, I unlocked the simple deadbolt set in a steel frame. The switch for the bare bulb that hung two feet down from the middle of the nine-foot ceiling was just inside the door. I had put an adapter in the light socket so I could run an extension cord over to my old desk where a driftwood lamp was rigged up. I turned it on and climbed up a paint-spattered aluminum step ladder to twist the overhead bulb off. I hate overhead lights, and now the door switch would just turn on the desk lamp. I wiped the dust off the desk and an old metal folding chair and went to work.

It didn't take long. After a trip to the grubby little sink I was left with less than a half-full mickey of Scotch. I poured in the GHB, leaving only a few drops — enough for analysis. I put the vial in with the stuff I was going to give to Robbie and carefully slid the doctored Scotch back into the thick brown paper bag from the liquor store. I still wasn't quite sure what I was going to do with it. I had picked the same brand Dagmar had fished from her purse, but only out of the sense of symmetry I developed as a caterer. It would probably be too much to hope that Ananah not only liked Scotch, but enjoyed stealing it from Dagmar even more.

My shotgun was broken down and lying in two pieces in the box it had come in. I kept it behind the false panel I had installed to keep it, and a few other items of value, hidden in case security was breached. You never know in these old places. I put the same care and attention into this that I did in building my restaurant — so if you weren't looking for it it would be tough to spot. At the time, I was pissed off at the introduction of the GST. It all but drove my business into the ground, wiping out ten years of considerable effort. I decided to get into an enterprise in which the collection of tax imposed by a bunch of drunken idiots would be the least of my concerns. I mean, I was already a criminal just for smoking the stuff. However, thanks to the brilliant idea of subscription lists and direct delivery I didn't ever use my secret hideaway to store grass.

I opened the box. It was all there: the stock, trigger, breech, magazine and pump in one piece, and the thirty-inch barrel in the other. Looking at it made me nostalgic for the hunt, for an excuse to shoot. I put my personal stash of grass and roofies beside the two boxes of assorted shotgun shells I had collected over the years. One was full — twenty-five in all — mostly Number 2s and Number 4s for pheasant and chicken; the other was almost full, and had lighter loads, smaller pellets, Number 5s and Number 6s for ruffies and Hungarian partridge. Beside them were two slender boxes that held five shells each of heavy lead slugs used for deer. Add a couple of boxes of double ought buckshot and a person could do a fair amount of damage. Maybe I'll get one box for the collection.

I was back at the car in fifteen minutes. I waved to Ray who was at the far end of the vacant lot next door with Gandhi. He was doing up his fly. I was clean, or I would be, after I passed the large vial I had assembled to Robbie. The only thing incriminating in my possession would then be the roach I planned to smoke on my way to Dagmar's. By eightish I would be a sober, upstanding citizen — more or less.

"Sorry," said Ray breathlessly, "wiz time."

"Let's go see if Weilander is home," I said. And we piled into the car, again with me as chauffeur alone in the front seat. "I like it back here," is all Ray said when I invited him up to first class.

We headed west, across town, and our route took us past the police station. I kept my eyes straight ahead — Joe Innocent with a hairy freak and a large, ugly dog wearing a turban in the back seat. Nobody gave us a second look. I was retracing a shortened version of last night's ride with Weilander to see if Kuyek's car was still there.

Fortunately, my cop radar was on yellow alert. It beeped just as I was about to turn left off 15th Avenue and come up behind Kuyek's position. An ambulance and two cop cars were bottlenecking the far end of the block. I pulled over, still on 15th, and parked by the alley.

"Maybe I'll take a quick stroll and peek down the block," I said to Ray. "Stay in the car."

"Yass. Be careful," he cautioned.

I waited for an old Chevy to pass before I opened my door. It was full of Indian kids pointing towards the action and laughing about something. Just as I reached for the door a shadowy figure burst from the alley and ran for our car. It took a second to register who it was. Gandhi began to growl, but stopped as the front passenger door flew open.

Weilander jumped in and slammed the door shut. "Man, am I glad to see you guys," he said, ducking below the dash. "Now let's get the fuck outta here!"

chapter twelve

The supermarket was closed. The stores on both sides of it were closed. Only the laundromat remained open. A few cars were backed up to it and a handful more were parked at random in the lot. Could be my watch was fast — we hadn't synchronized like proper commandos — but Robbie was late.

Despite all the space in front of the Safeway, I parked a block away in the even larger lot beside Holy Rosary Cathedral. I left Weilander in the care of Ray and Gandhi and told them to stay close to the car, that I wouldn't wait if I was in a hurry and that they would only have themselves to blame.

Weilander hardly even heard me. It was more than his being rousted again by Shpak. Apparently he had just missed Ray and me by fifteen minutes or he could have come to the beach. He had walked back to his place from Lenore's.

"And, Jeez, there I was up on the next block, minding my own business, when I got sandbagged by this huge cloud of fucking garlic. Fuck, did it stink! 'Specially with fart smell mixed in with it. I mean, Jeez, when you're ripping the guts out of a bird you expect it, eh? You kinda get ready for it, 'specially if it's been in the sun a while. So

I look and it's that fat fucker, Kuyek, sleeping in the car. I'm thinking, Jeez, he's spying on me. But then I say fuck him and I go home anyway. I'm beat. Didn't get much sleep last night. Next thing I know I'm crashing on the couch until I get stabbed by that loose spring. Did I tell you guys to watch out for that? Gotta get a new cushion.

"So now I can't sleep. I go down to the basement. I'm doing a badger for the museum, eh. Fucking place was a mess. Shit everywhere. What the fuck happened here, I'm wondering?" And at this point he looked right at me and then Ray. We wisely kept silent, knowing that verbal momentum was an irresistable force with Weilander.

"I just get it cleaned up and my workbench back into nice shape and the phone rings. Gotta get an extension down there. So I run upstairs and it's for you," he said, turning to me. "Something about a clinic in Toronto. I took a number. Oh fuck, it's still by the phone. Man, she had a great voice. Oh yeah, says it's urgent. Jeez, sorry."

I told him I couldn't call until the next day anyway, so not to worry. Ray gave me a sharp look, but I ignored him.

"Hope it isn't contagious, whatever it is, eh," he laughed and hurried on. "So no sooner do I put the phone down when I hear a siren coming down College and stopping real close. I take a look from the front step and see them put the stretcher in the ambulance. I knew it was Fat Boy, eh. Looked like a dropcloth over a weather balloon. Then I saw Shpak get out of one of the cop cars so I took off up the alley. When I saw you guys, Jeez, even Ray looked good." Catching himself he made a rare stab at politesse and said to Ray, "No offence, eh?"

"None taken." Ray bowed his head slightly.

What else was going on, I wondered? To make small talk, really, I asked, "So how's Glennie and Lenore?"

"Uh, okay," was all he said.

"Ananah get home okay?"

"Yup," was his one syllable reply.

I'll get it out of him later. One toke and the bastard

would be mine. In the meantime, where the fuck is Robbie?

I tried to think of anything but the call from Toronto. Never once have I responded to something urgent to be told, "Yes, you are a winner!" Urgent is just another word for bad news. Unless it really isn't urgent: in which case it's another word for pissoff. Either way, it fucks with your digestion.

Speaking of which, on the side street across from the Safeway lot stood the 'Q', a.k.a. the 'QTR', or, as its fifties era neon sign proclaims, the Quality Tea Room. Like the Vesta Lunch in Toronto, it serves a cast-iron, boilerplate cuisine of plain, decent food in generous portions at prices that harken back to another decade. And, like the Only in Vancouver, you might find anyone in there at any time — including the mayor. It was one of the last of a type of chrome, vinyl and formica establishments that proliferated in the west and, as such, the "Q" might well stand for quintessential. I hadn't expected it, but there were still a few people inside.

"Jeez, you're right, eh, it is open," said a familiar voice behind me. I only jumped a little.

"Yass. They're trying out new hours," said an even more familiar voice.

I turned to face them. Of the two, Ray could sit still longer but neither of them would win an award for staying in place just for the sake of mere waiting. It was a wonder they didn't get here ahead of me.

"I haven't eaten since this morning," said Weilander, handing me the car keys. "I left the windows open just a hair," he added, looking at me significantly.

"Time for din-dins," chimed Ray. "But we'll stay out here." He said, pointing to a battleship-brown picnic table, the kind you see at provincial parks, that was permanently stationed outside the Q.

"They don't have pizza, Ray," I said, although for all I knew they well might now.

"I know. Just a little something until we can get to Georgie's."

Weilander and I sat at a deuce by the window and ordered five 'Big Mike's', four of them to go. It seems that canine vegetarianism was a desired state, like Satori, but by no means canonical law. According to Ray the Omnivorous at least.

"Last one to finish has to share," said Ray to Gandhi. I hurried back inside. It was five to eight, getting dark, and still no Robbie.

Now wouldn't be the time to tell Weilander that he had had a visitor today, one that I was supposed to be having dinner with right about now. I also kept quiet about Janey, and the fact that Robbie was looking to warn him about Shpak. He seemed inordinately focussed on his food. Not chatty at all. I watched him eat.

Two booths over an old guy, chain smoking, started coughing up a lung. Really hacking away, finally horking up a snotball and swallowing it in relief. With a start I realized that I knew the guy — Dave something or other — who was maybe two years older than I. Still a cowboy I see, same wardrobe anyway. Why do I know him?

"Hey, Slickie, who's that?"

Weilander turned to look. "That? That's Davey Williams. You should remember him."

"How's that?"

"Warrior Williams. Don't you remember kicking the shit out of him one night at the bar?"

"Oh yeah. Fuck. That guy. Now there's an evening I don't want to remember. Besides I didn't kick the shit out of him. I hardly touched the guy."

"Davey! Shit, how's it goin', man?" Weilander blurted, before I could shut him up. "I didn't see you there, eh."

"Huh?" said Davey in a tired voice, squinting to see who had dragged him out of his reverie. "Oh, hiya, Ace, been a while."

Davey was looking far less robust than on the night of our encounter, years and years ago. His face was lined and grey, his mustache drooped, and an air of sorrow hung round his head like a wreath of Sunday morning hurtin' songs. He was always a hard-headed guy, a hippie that dressed like a cowboy; the kind that not only read Casteneda's "Teachings of Don Juan" but would forever quote it. Some were warriors, most weren't. Davey, however, was damned well sure he was a warrior, a major warrior, which is why things didn't always work out so good because he was surrounded by all these wimps and non-warriors who, nevertheless, through some unfortunate spiritual alignment, had decision-making power over him.

The ladies sure loved him, though. He was a skinny six-footer and always had a beauty on his arm. They seemed to tire quickly, except for the real quirky ones who lingered on a year or two longer, marrying him just to get even and return some of the grief.

He was between wives that night at the bar. Weilander and I had just joined a couple of ladies by invitation and were reasonably hopeful of making a complete evening of it when the warrior intruded. Before you could say "shaman" he was preaching and dipping his fingers into our beer, flicking it at us to make a point. Unfortunately, my restraint muscle goes all slack when I drink, and before I could help myself I was pouring a glass of draught into his lap; slowly, deliberately, and looking him in the eye while I did it. It was a trick I had learned from Weilander who, small as he is, is nobody you'd want to fuck with. Hard as the prairie, that one.

"I forgive you," Davey said, looking down at his soaked crotch. "I am a warrior and I forgive you. Do you forgive me?"

"Go fuck yourself," I said. And we walked out the side door to the alley with Davey holding the door wide, beckoning and bowing in a most courtly fashion.

At this point sobriety made a brief entrance, just long enough to verify that, yep, I was terrified all right. Many an evening we had seen the warrior enact this drama and return to the bar a short while later, all smiles and blowing on his knuckles. I was so scared that when he warned me about his karate skills and that, reluctantly, he might have to use them, I almost collapsed on the spot. Then he did an annoying thing.

Open-handed, he reached over and gave me a playful slap on the side of the head before he crouched into a fighting stance and began circling. He grinned, feinting this way and that. I charged him in a rage, catching him in the stomach with my head. There was a flurry of blows and I remembered as we went down to, above all else, be the guy on top when we landed. Moose McAlpine taught me that lesson, one that I permanently wear on my lower lip.

I was not without philosophic resource myself. I figured Lao Tzu could clean Don Juan's clock any day of the week. "Gravity is the root of grace, the mainstay of all speed," he says. Tall guys usually discount this, forgetting that the physics of punching up are more favourable than the physics of punching down. When the dust settled, the warrior was on his back. My left hand was wrapped around his nuts, my knee was in his stomach and my right hand was trying to rip the hair off the top of his head. I was appalled by my savagery, as usual, but fear will do that to you.

Before I could tear his throat out with my teeth, which is what I had in mind, I let him go. I got to my feet, apologized, and went back inside. Bite? You bet. Kick, scratch, claw; anything to avoid being hit. I hate being hit: loathe it, despise it. Not because of the pain, because of the indignity. I'm the other end of the spectrum from guys that enjoy a good scrap. I am basically a coward; low down, sniveling and craven. So my approach is to never finish a guy off. Never push too far. Leave him somewhere near redemption but shy of resolve, unless you have no choice. The lessons of violence are cut and dried. I wish it were so with sex, but there you're up against a different animal entirely. With any luck.

The warrior and I were buddy buddy for a while after

that evening. I never got over being more than a bit uncomfortable in his presence and I took care to thank him for the lesson he had imparted, to his bewilderment.

"That you, Frank? You're looking good."

"You too, Davey."

"No I'm not." He said and got up abruptly, leaving without saying another word.

"Strange guy," shrugged Weilander, returning to his burger.

There was a small crowd in the Q, hardy and ancient smokers for the most part, defying the statistics, god bless 'em. I had only given them a cursory glance prior to seeing Davey. That explains why I missed seeing her. In fact, I was fascinated and distracted by a skinny, stoop-shouldered guy, mid-forties, horn-rimmed glasses with what looked like a hearing aid built into the frame. He was intently focussed on a book called Ventriloquism Made Easy. His lips were moving as he read.

The voice squealed out above the low-level hum of the diner. It came from the last booth in the corner, where I had noted a young couple side by side, their backs toward us, nuzzling and pawing one another.

"Eww, that's disgusting!" the girl said. Then, not quite as loud, but loud enough, "Let's go try it, okay?"

Ananah slid out of the booth first and I realized as I got ready to greet Donald that I didn't want to see him just yet. It had been over two years, but it was still too soon. My mind said: be happy to see him. My stomach did a flip and told me to hide. There was misery there, and I wanted to avoid it.

In a flash, I could see that doing Ananah in before the wedding had less to do with saving him and more to do with providing a mechanism by which I could avoid seeing Donald until I was ready. As good a reason as any. No Ananah, no wedding, no need to put in an appearance. The question of paternity could gather dust.

The coward's way out. Yes.

That was it! I needed more time to deal with all the unresolved issues that had been stirred up of late. My hidden agenda — hidden to me, that is — was revealed: I'm sick of the little bastard, of all the guilt trips being laid on me. I need time, lots of it, to sort stuff out. The wedding was squeezing me in the way he always squeezed me to get what he wants — a tactic he learned at his mummy's knee.

After all, it's hardly like me to be running around assisting in somebody's demise. Not like me at all. What was I thinking? I mean, there was the question of grandchildren. Not only how unfortunately stupid they would be, but that each would be like a little hot coal of guilt designed to torture me. Why? Because I would hate what caring for the little bastards could do to me. Her kids, my grandchildren. I could not redeem myself with Donald through his children. No second chance for Frankie boy. And her type would always get pregnant to seal the deal. Fuck.

I could just see the back of his head and shoulders as he slid out. He looked thinner and he'd let his hair grow long again. Oh well. I'll just deal with it. I looked to see if Weilander had noticed Ananah. He had a french fry held suspended between his rigid fingers, frozen, a look of dismay on his face which was reddening by the second as he stared at her. It was the face of a guilty man. Ananah seemed to hesitate before catching herself and fake smiling at us. I don't think it was because of Weilander that she faltered. The thin-faced, pock-marked, sneering scuzzball who got out of the booth wasn't Donald. Now Weilander and I were twins, bookends with open mouths.

The word "Daddy" rang out like fingernails on a blackboard. "How sweet to see yew," she said, with all the sincerity of a telemarketer. Then she turned to her sidekick, the ferret, handed him a twenty, and said, "Pay up and I'll meet you outside."

It looked like the hooker was giving orders to the pimp. In fact, the pimp almost said something, but caught himself and sauntered by with a smirk playing at the corner of his mouth. Later, pal, was my reaction.

Just for fun I said, "Hi, Ananah. You remember Mr. Weilander." I pointed to the red-faced gent in question.

"If yew say so," she replied, acting as if she had no notion of who he was, where she had met him, or why she should care. Weilander looked relieved, if a bit offended. The ego is always first to bob to the surface after ducking a close call.

"Donald not back yet?" I asked.

"He'll be here tomorrow, or the next day after that. Ew, I'm sew excited."

"Yes, I can see that," I said, looking pointedly at the thug who was pocketing the change from the cashier.

"Oh, that's my cousin from Toronto. We're very close. He's coming to the wedding tew."

"Well, you can never have enough family," I said.

"Guess not. Anyway, I have to run." Then, lowering her voice and sticking her ass in Weilander's face, she leaned towards me and said, "Yew haven't forgotten about that treat, have yew?"

"The one I promised last night?"

"Yeah."

"As a matter of fact I was just about to step outside and have a little snort of Scotch. Perhaps you and your cousin would like to join me."

"Scotch? Ew, that's not what I ..."

"No. No. I'll have the other later. This is just a drink to celebrate Donald's homecoming. Whaddya say, daughter?"

"Oh okay. Omar will like it."

"Your cousin?"

"Yeah. But let's go," she snapped, giving her rude, impatient side some slack.

"So you remember last night, then?"

"What a question. Course I dew." Furrowing her brow she added, "Most of it anyway." And as she moved towards the door I caught her giving Weilander a playful poke in the shoulder on the way by. He turned all red again; redder, if anything.

This slyness was something new to me, something to be watched in the short term. More than ever I was hoping for as short a term as possible. Stupid, blonde grandchildren were one thing; endowing them with a nasty slyness quite another. No point in hoping they might at least bedevil Dagmar. She's not particularly fond of children, and wouldn't be much affected by their antics. I would though, for however long I'd be around.

I had been using my jacket for a purse. I grabbed it and followed Ananah. I told Weilander I'd be right back and gave him a poke the way Ananah had. He almost said fuck off. I could tell. The mickey in my jacket pocket bumped against my leg.

I was going to signal Ray to stay put, but he was busy hugging Gandhi and didn't take any notice of me. Cousin Omar, surprise surprise, bore no resemblance to the bitch whatsoever. Actually, he resembled a rat with bad teeth, and looked vaguely familiar. He offered a nod and a "Yeah, man" when introduced: a rounder with a capital R. Sure he'd have a drink. "Why the fuck not?" Staring at me up and down like he could take me easy. I grabbed the bottle by the cap between my first two fingers as you would a cigar and offered it to Omar first.

"After you. You can see I already beat you to it." I pointed to the partly filled bottle.

"Whatever," he sneered and reached for the Scotch. There was a tattoo of a devil on the soft mound of flesh between his thumb and forefinger. No swastika, at least. A classy guy.

We stepped behind the tree in front of the building next door. Omar was about to unscrew the cap when he stiffened. He was looking over my shoulder. On point. Watching a police car turn slowly into the Safeway lot.

"Gotta go," he said, extending the bottle in my direction.

"Keep it," I said. "Have a couple on me."

He shrugged without saying a word and grabbed Ananah roughly by the arm. He tucked the Scotch into her purse as he steered her up the street and around the corner. Not fast. Not slow. Efficient. I walked over to the picnic table. I'll have to trust in the lord that the whiskey will find its way.

"Who was that with Ananah?" Ray asked as the police car crept to our side of the lot. I hoped it was Robbie.

"She says it's cousin Omar. They're very close," I added, trying to imitate her stupid voice.

"Like kissing cousins," said Ray.

"Yep. And I'm beginning to see that she might have a big family." Only Donald could be so blind, I thought.

"Gandhi sure didn't like him."

"No? Doesn't surprise me."

"I had to physically restrain him, for goodness sakes."

"I'm sorry I missed that," I said, to lighten up the Ray-man.

"He looks more like Shpak's cousin. Except for the hair."

"Well, Ray, if he's thirsty he might not be around for long."

"That would be good," Ray said, without really getting what I was driving at. Although, with Ray you never know. Here's hoping Omar takes Ananah with him. She was really starting to annoy me.

When Robbie stepped out of the car I looked for Weilander. He was no longer at the window. I asked Ray.

"That's a good question, um, maybe he's in the bathroom. Or maybe he went out the back door."

"There is no back door," I said, not ever having seen one.

"There's always a back door," Ray insisted.

"Gee, Ray, I'll remember you said that."

"See that you do," he admonished. We both laughed, neither of us exactly knowing why.

"What's so funny?" asked Robbie when he got to the table.

"Philosophy," I said, explaining.

"There's two," Robbie said.

"Two what?" I asked.

"Back doors. One through the kitchen and one through that doorway off the courtyard."

"Shit," I said, worried that I lost him. "I haven't told Weilander anything yet. He's too busy being freaked out about Kuyek."

"You heard then?" Robbie asked.

"Sorta. Ray, tell Robbie what we know and I'll check the bathroom."

"Okaay."

The cash counter was just inside the entrance. A prim, disapproving sort of woman in nondescript, washed-out, old-lady clothes stood resolvedly by the register holding our bill. Above her frizzy, grey, permed head a halo of hand-printed religious quotes on recipe cards, exhorting me to repent and find Jesus, were tacked to the wall, beside row upon row of cigarettes for sale. You had to love that about the Q; divergent cultures existing side by side in harmony. Besides, to ban smoking with that particular clientele would be like having most of the customers dying all at once instead of one by one at decent intervals.

"Your friend tried to run out the back," she sniffed. "Now he's in the bathroom."

"Allow me, madam." I handed her some cash. "And be sure to keep a little extra for the collection on Sunday," I added, knowing how much it would irritate her.

Her lips were tightly pursed as she rang up our bill, making a point of counting out all my change.

"C'mon, Slickie, get outta there. It's only Robbie," I said, pounding on the door of the Men's when I found it locked.

The door opened about six inches, uncorking a ferocious stench. My knees buckled. A head with horn-rimmed glasses peered out from a sitting position and the ventriloquist said, "I'll be done in a minute if you don't mind." Then, as if to show me his lessons had worked, a disembodied voice came from behind me.

"Fuck, get him to close that door!" said Weilander, emerging from the Ladies'.

"I only got a couple of minutes," Robbie said, when we were all huddled at the picnic table. "First, Kuyek. Preliminary reports indicate heart attack, but the lady that found him said his face was blue, so I don't know, he mighta choked. There was a chunk of gristle caught in his throat, and a half-eaten sausage in his hand. One of those big garlic coils from the co-op." Robbie paused, waiting for the snickering and snorting to die down. "You guys about done?" He tried to preserve a shred of dignity for a fallen comrade.

"Death by kielbossa. You don't see a lot of that," I said, setting off another round. Even Robbie joined in.

"Jeez, that's great," said Weilander. "I mean, hard luck and all, but that lets me off the hook."

"Nope," I said.

"Au contraire," Ray added.

"Not exactly," confirmed Robbie, and he told Weilander about Janey, and that they were still waiting on forensics. "Shpak may or may not be involved, and he may or may not want your ass, Slickie. Find a place and hole up. One, maybe two days."

"She was a sweet kid," Weilander said, genuinely moved. "Leg or no, eh? Always smiling." Then he snapped out of it. "Yeah, I'll stay at Lenore's I guess."

"Someone should stay at your house, Slick," I said. "Keep an eye on things. Make it look like you're there."

"Jeez, yeah. Good idea."

"Give Ray your key, then."

"Ray? Where are you going to be?"

"Here and there," I said, staring him down until he finally handed Ray the key.

chapter thirteen

The photograph, clipped from a magazine, was a cropped frontal nude of a female torso that ran from just under the rib cage to mid thigh. Engaging the eye, dead centre, was a silky dark triangle of curls — and a shiny, healthy goatee it was, if a trifle neat. Personally, I prefer a bit of pubic unruliness, a touch of rebellion, where tiny tufts escape the stricture of bikini bottoms and wave like weeds outside a circus tent while under the big top, vibrating to the roar of lions, cavorting clowns and damsels dancing on the backs of dappled Appaloosas, the show that must go on goes on.

Also missing, sadly waxed or airbrushed away, is the lovely hedge of softer hair that flies true as an arrow from the inverted base of the delta along the gently rounded tummy to the bullseye of the navel. This is a line with much to say, no two alike. I believe you can decipher the pattern of follicular squiggles, like reading tea leaves. For character, not for prophecy. Hairoglyphics.

It is a colour photograph, of course; the skin without blemish, the body full and enticing. The photo could stand on its own without the gratuitous, thorny, long-stemmed red rose draped across the stomach, dragging us down to the level of cheap girly mag, its obvious origin. The image has been glued to the front of a folded piece of 20-pound bond, chopped down to greeting card size. It is centered and takes up one third of the page. Above the photo is the caption: PANDORA'S BOX.

Let's not consider here euphemistic terms for vagina. "Box" is one I have never been particularly fond of, reeking, as it does, of ignorance, of low-browed men of limited expressive means, of those who see women solely in terms of the sex act with which they are only semi-conversant, and whose most sophisticated advocates have attained the level of mastery of two grunts and a sigh before rolling off into a deep snore. (Adolescent boys are exempt from this, being inclined to put any sort of name to the mystery in hopes of delving into its secrets. As are bull dykes, who are entitled to name any goddamned part of their bodies any fucking way they want. Or not.) The crime of vulgarity is not at issue.

Perhaps the crime of misogyny is. But I'd like to invoke the notwithstanding clause to serve the cause of metaphor. Damned good metaphor. Right on the money. Pandora, the first woman, was made for Zeus for the express purpose of punishing man. And Pandora's Box, which is to say any source of great and unexpected troubles, is looking pretty fine in this picture, despite the tawdry flora.

The handbuilt card was from Poole. In lieu of writing letters, we exchanged silly missives, or sculptures. We called it Junk Mail. In this case, he was responding to my anguish during a particularly brutal romantic severance.

I was hurting big time when Pandora's Box arrived in the mail. Tearing myself away from the cover photo, which bore an uncanny resemblance, torso-wise, to the object of my misplaced affection, I opened the card. Centred on the inner page was another photograph, much smaller, one inch square, in black and white: a headshot of a toothless old granny, glaring fiercely at the camera. She was some ugly, her face all scrunched up and a chin that stuck out like Popeye's. Under this photo was a tab that, when lifted, revealed the word PANDORA.

And there you have it. The recovery process began.

Donald wouldn't get it. He'd understand the joke all right, the surface, but not the core. If it were explained to him he'd say he got it, but he still wouldn't, mainly because it would hold no interest for him. It's out of his comfort zone. He can see Ananah's box, what with her waving it around all the time, but he can't see Ananah. Yes, I know, I should talk, love is blind, and it's none of my business anyway.

One last time I would like to help Donald in a way I didn't get myself. One last time, because his cry was genuine, and not his everyday, run-of-the-mill whining. The guy is in pain but I can't get past these fucking bitches to lend a hand. Find a way to stop the wedding, I thought. Buy him some time to sort things out. Do it unobtrusively so it's his solution, not anyone else's. Actually, I see now that Dagmar poses a greater danger to Donald than Ananah. He's willfully blind to the blonde goat, but absolutely helpless against his mummy. She will always be there, keeping him close so she won't be left alone.

Donald, to his credit, has been a difficult dolly for Dagmar to keep in line. He has learned her tricks; they're two of a kind. Unfortunately, he appears to prefer his strokes on the negative side. So his calls were about that as much as anything. I tried not to play the game, fuelling his anger. One time when he was eight and, in his mind, stuck with me for the summer, I made the alarming discovery that he couldn't sleep unless he had a fight before bedtime. Let him read a comic, chat about the day, sit with him for a while, and he'd be up past midnight. Get in a hassle, order him to bed and he'd be out like a light in seconds, still muttering imprecations — gone for twelve hours. I took to inventing arguments so he could get the requisite amount of rest. I never felt good about it.

His calls — really, there were only a few — were of the wake-up variety. Here it is, twenty years later give or take, and I'm transported into a past where little Donald, already saying "fuck" for grandma, is having a problem with beddy-byes. It all began with a demand for money. Not a large sum and, even though I was temporarily in a cash flow crisis, not unmanageable. Nevertheless, demands beget different responses than requests.

"Did unemployment cut you off again?" I asked.

"No."

"Still bartending on the sly?"

"Yeah."

"Groceries low?"

"No."

"So why do you need this exact amount of money?"

"Lookfuck," he says, in his endearing way of adding "fuck" to words as if it were a suffix, "I just want it okay? You're supposed to be my fucking father. How dare you question me!"

"Sorry. Just making sure you aren't in some kind of trouble. Is anybody going to break your legs if you don't come up with the cash?"

"Fuck you. Why are you being such an asshole? I want the money. I'm your sonfuck. How often do I ever ask you for anything? You owe it to me. Just send it for fucksakes."

At this point I'm thinking he's strung out on coke or something. His anger would stay with me for days, rumbling through my digestive system, substituting itself for sleep. But I resisted telling him that he's always asking for something, always in need. That the only time I hear from him is when the need is dire. And, that as far as I can see, it is a need without bottom, one that changes at will but can never be filled, stretching out until the end of all our days. And I reflect upon the fact that he is an adult, and this is not adult behaviour.

"So you're okay, you're not in any trouble?" I ask, thinking of the insurance fraud, or the assault charge for hitting that girl, or how he relentlessly plundered the restaurant.

"Lookfuck, I just want to get ahead a little, okay? What's

the big fucking deal?

"I'll think about it. See what I can do."

"Yeah. Fuck. Whatever." He hung up.

On the off chance he was in trouble or wasn't eating, although he had never been shy about describing the exact breadth and depth of his miseries, I sent him half the sum he had demanded. Disturbing as that call was, it was mere bagatelle compared to his next, the one that began "Yeah, ya fuck ya," the one that I thought was an obscene phone call until I realized it was Donald. After the third time I got call display. Now I only pick up if I know who's calling.

Two years later he came to see me. He spent most of his time in the bar. Nevertheless, I saw it as a conciliatory visit. A few months later he showed up with Ananah. Shortly thereafter, presumably because of my reaction to her — guarded though extremely polite — the calls began again. "Why can't you be happy for me, you fucker?" And so on.

Just when you think you have the good name of Frankenstein restored to its former glory, your son turns up as one of the villagers, intent on burning down the castle. The vacant look and the pitchfork are more disturbing than the fire.

There was a definite nip in the air as I walked to Dagmar's, and I was glad I had my jacket. I didn't phone ahead to excuse my tardiness, preferring to take my lumps on arrival. This dinner date was her trip anyway, not my idea. I wouldn't even have a relationship with her, such as it is, were it not for Donald. But I do need to know what she was up to. Robbie had his roofies, Weilander was off to Lenore's, Ray and Gandhi were walking to Georgie's for a proper meal, and I was staring down the barrel of a long, cold evening with the Queen of the Dollies. Oh boy.

You should stay away from pot if you're heading into a downer. Who needs to heighten a sense of despair? However, since I was still buzzing from the beach, but fading fast, I fired up the roach. I took three good tokes and ate the rest, stubbing it out first. Not like Moyer, who ingests it burning coal and all. I keep hoping the bastard will burn himself, but he never has.

Man, this is good smoke. Things were getting just a bit too serious.

The lights of the houses offered warmth as I floated through my old neighborhood. On every block I passed there was at least one home where I would be known if not welcome. But I walked as a stranger taking it in for the first time. I don't live here any more. My house is no longer my house, and the new people are my old neighbor's neighbors. There is no trace of me here. On the day I moved I vanished like a stone dropped into a pond. There was a splash, ripples spread and then all was still. Now I meander softly through the afterlife, my footsteps hidden in the high wind's rustle of the leaves.

In one of Time's ageless tricks, I arrived at Dagmar's far too late for her and way too soon for me. I could have walked for hours. Days even. I stood outside for a while before knocking.

"Jesus fucking Christ, you took your time."

"Couldn't be helped," I said. "But I'm here now, so let's go."

"Jesus, I need a minute to get ready. You know that, for fucksakes."

Oh, I knew all right. Now it was my turn to wait. At least she was minus a devil dog and I wouldn't have to pose unconcernedly, secretly in terror, while some vicious beast sniffed my crotch — it's so hard to cross your legs standing up and still look dignified. You know, and the dog knows, how diaphanous the veil of restraint is: a mere wisp of whimsy, tattered around the edges, standing between you and doggie's teeth around your nuts.

The smell hit me as I walked through the glassed-in porch. It wasn't overpowering, but it was entrenched, hanging in the air in layers like Neapolitan ice cream. Moving through them stirred everything up, and vaguely familiar odours mixed with those more exotic, in a minor olfactory assault. The bass note was a mix of wet fur, kibble and old dog blanket. Mid-range was an empty liquor bottle fruitiness, softened by stale tobacco smoke. And, upon entering the house, it was all topped off by the pungency of cat.

A small room just off the front entrance smelled vaguely of chicken coop. I was startled by a high-pitched shriek as I walked past the doorway, and I looked in time to see a tiny blue ball of feathers collapse and fall from a swinging perch. It landed in a heap at the bottom of a doorless bird cage. The little thing lay there, on its back, legs in the air twitching briefly, before it went still. The floor of the room was covered with old newspapers. There was a small wooden table and a stack of unframed oil paintings leaning against one wall. Everything was splotched with blobs of birdshit.

"Looks like your budgie just died," I said, not knowing whether to laugh or be concerned.

"Mr. Wacko?" she laughed. "No, he'll come around in a minute." Then in the baby talk she reserves for animals Dagmar explained, "Him just likes to thump him's little stump." In a normal voice she said, "He likes to sit on his perch and masturbate himself with his beak but he falls off when he comes. He loses his grip." Back to baby talk she crooned, "Birdie, birdie," and poked at him through the bars. She was rewarded with a soft little peep and a stirring of feathers.

"Shadow! No. Sit!" Dagmar spoke from behind me while I watched the little blue guy dust himself off, get back on his perch, and start preening. I think he was preening. I turned to see there was a dog after all. Not big, but adequately sized.

As if to reinforce the feeling that I had stumbled onto the island of Dr. Moreau, it was one of the strangest animals I've ever seen. It looked like the offspring of a badger-hyena cross who'd mated with a wire-haired whippet. It was all black spots, bushy tri-coloured tail, dense grey-brindle coat and a long, narrow, whiskered charcoal snout. One eye was cold ice blue, the other a muddy brown. Dagmar held its collar as it strained and jumped toward me. It didn't bark, preferring instead to whine and gurgle.

"I think I'll wait outside" I said.

"Don't be silly," Dagmar said. "Jesus, Frank, you used to love dogs."

"Oh, that's a dog."

"Of course she is, don't be an asshole. She just wants to get close and smell you. Sit, Shadow," she said and whacked the dog on the rump to little avail. It still wanted at me.

"Bit neurotic, is she?"

"Well, Jesus Christ, you'd be neurotic too if you were blind and deaf. Just come here and let her smell you."

If I were a dog that was blind and deaf I'd be looking for a way to get shot, I thought, but I moved over to the dog and held out my hand. William Blake asks, "How do you know but ev'ry Bird that cuts the airy way, is an immense world of delight, clos'd (to you) by your senses five?" Well, I just met a bird that answers the question; as for Shadow, who could know? She went crazy with the first whiff and bit me. It was more of a nip, effected by the dog moving her teeth up and down rapidly like electric shears. Then she jumped up, jabbing my groin with her paws a couple of times. After that she settled down. This would be Dagmar's insurance dog, for when the others somehow ran away, or died, or got put down.

My mouth was dry from the roach, which is about the only unpleasant side effect of marijuana. That is, if you don't count the brief bout of paranoia that can occur around minute fifteen, which leaves as suddenly as it arrives if you don't dwell on it. I walked straight through to the kitchen and no beast assailed me, not even one in a blue uniform. I ran the tap and gulped a few cups of water. Why is it that kitty litter boxes are placed in the room where people prepare food? I can practically see the little bastards taking a shit while I'm eating. I can smell it. Must have a discussion with Ray about that.

"How about a wee drinkie, Frank?" Dagmar pointed to a bottle of Scotch. "I have to finish mine anyway." Her large tumbler was almost full.

"Actually, I wouldn't mind getting some food first. Kinda hungry," I said.

Given recent developments, tap water was all I dare drink at her house. Not only that, but on a counter by the sink, where an old radio was quietly sawing out some FM classical background music, I spotted candies and cigarettes beside a well-worn groove in the countertop. The divot was about the size of Dagmar's ass. She did her best work in the kitchen. It was like a fucking minefield in there.

"What a bastard, you keep me waiting and now you're in a hurry," she said almost playfully.

Now I'm really getting edgy. She, of course, picked up on my discomfort and was already mulling over the possibilities of what to do about it.

I made a break for the long living room. It had an old piano beside an older oak table at one end, and a big-screen TV at the other. A couch sat at midpoint in the room, facing the television. It was covered with animal hair, so I took one of the chairs around the table.

"So let's go," I said impatiently. Maybe I could provoke a hassle and storm out.

"All right," she said quietly, "just give me a minute." And glug went half her drink. It was un-Dagmar like to give in like that. Something was up. For one thing, I expected her to be roaring drunk by now. But she wasn't, at least not that I could see.

Dagmar went upstairs, presumably to apply the final coat of whatever was holding it all together. I sat there feeling uneasy, bothered by something I couldn't name, oppressed as usual by her environment. I imagined I heard whispering. Then it stopped. I tried to elevate my vibe by perusing the art work, about a hundred thousand dollar's worth. I was familiar with most of it; nearly all of which had been done by her father. At least the bastard could paint.

The main piece, accorded the place of honour above the mantel over the fireplace, was a nude, obviously of a younger Dagmar. It was one I had never seen. She was fully reclined, with her head, at three-quarters profile, in the foreground. The rest of her body angled slightly away to the right. Her left knee was raised and her right leg stretched out. One arm, the left, was draped across her stomach, while the other dangled a wrist over the edge of her place of repose. Her eyes — liquid, expressive — were cast shyly downward.

If you approached the woman lying there from the other side of the painting, from the back, you would be staring at seduction writ large. The way it was presented, frontally, her modesty held you at bay. The flesh tones were sumptuous and, drawing you in even further, one nipple was erect while the other was partially concealed. The upper part of her pubic hair could be seen, dead centre, dark and delicious. I had heard about this painting: a minor stir was created when Dagmar posed nude for her father shortly after our divorce. It was an incredible work that said more about the artist than the subject. It was sexy, joyous and sensual. She would never look so good.

Never mind the many sessions it must have taken to pose for the painting, and the thoughts that fleeted through the two solitudes occupying the studio. I mean, it's tempting to speculate, very tempting, and would no doubt produce several amusing narratives. What struck home to me, very forcefully, was that it was an idealized portrait of his daughter, one that captured, perhaps, an aspect of her — but nothing near the truth.

But now, I saw truth. The truth is that for too many years I have idealized Donald instead of having a good look at who he really is. To stretch the Pandora thing, I've been looking at the box, not Donald.

Oh oh, it's happening. Much as I am grateful for the revelation, every time I get near these people the downer starts. I'm getting an inkling why at least. People, I'm sure, enter this room, take in the oils, and acrylics, and watercolours, and woodcuts, and pen-and-ink drawings, and never notice the clutter. The walls are a shrine to Daddy, but also proclaim Dagmar's identity. Donald's as well, to a lesser extent. "This is who I am," they say. "This is why we are better than ordinary folks." None of her work is present. There are stacks of videos piled on top of and beside the blank TV, plants in need of attention, fluff balls in the corners, an old book case with old books. Everything in this room is from the past, including me.

"I'm ready," she hollered from the landing, not being so far gone that she could no longer make an entrance. Dutifully, I watched her sweep down the stairs. She was still dressed in layers, but the cardigan was newer. Rose-coloured spots adorned her cheeks. Her eyelids were painted dark, matching the faint rings below them.

"Looking good," I said. It was pretty much mandatory. Need forced her to ignore my perfunctory tone.

"Thank you," she said, modestly batting her glue-ons. Trying, but missing by quite a margin, to match the painting.

The final flurry of activity involved downing the last of her drink, issuing a small burp followed by a cutesy "I do beg your pardon," and sweeping candy, cigarettes and keys into her bag. A small clink indicated a glass object within its folds.

Dinner was to be at Myta's and did I remember it? "Vividly," I replied. Upon leaving, Shadow lunged once and missed. Mr. Wacko was preening more rapidly now, ignoring our exit. A raccoon-sized tabby with one ear rushed in when we opened the door, scaring the shit out of me and taking a swipe at the dog. I practically ran down the walk and waited at the curb.

"Jesus, you really are hungry," she said. "Are you driving?"

"I walked."

"Good. We can take mine," she said, leaving her in

control.

Hers was an old half-ton with a camper top, both of which had once been white a hundred dings and dents ago. It had a four-speed floor shift and if you were to substitute gasoline for kitty litter it would smell just like her house. I sat on a hairy blanket as she ground the gears all the way downtown. Dagmar opted for a spot in the middle of a near empty government lot beside Myta's. There was only one other car in the vicinity and she managed to hit it solidly with her bumper.

"That fucking asshole!" she said, suddenly furious and in dead earnest. "Imagine parking there like that."

At her house, and during the drive downtown, I had almost felt compassion for her. It is the one thing we can afford our enemies. But with Dagmar, compassion is always a mistake. She will find a way to impale you on your own kindness. Before you know what hit you you'll be nursing her sick cat while she spends the weekend in Rio.

The cat will shit in your shoes.

We walked across the lot. She was all chatty again, and I gathered we were about to die over some exquisite dessert. As we got to the sidewalk, tires screeched irritatingly close. A plain grey Chev with a red and blue light in the rear window backed up quickly and stopped beside us. The lone driver stared at us from behind the wheel.

"You fucker! You bastard!" screamed Dagmar, giving him the finger.

Shpak got out of the car.

chapter fourteen

Shpak stood beside the driver's door and leaned on the roof, keeping the car between him and us. He was in plain clothes, wearing a light-coloured jacket and shirt with dark pants. But just as the car was obviously an unmarked police vehicle, Shpak had cop stamped plainly on his face. Eyes that are trained to see everyone as a potential felon have a certain predatory look. Even Robbie has it to a degree, but his is tempered by an essentially non-judgmental nature. He doesn't try to bore a hole in you like Shpak.

"Where the fuck were you last night?" Dagmar hollered after her introductory harangue.

"Never mind where I was. What did you do to Roman?"

It was the first close look I had at the guy who was, probably, Dagmar's about to be ex-boyfriend. Although you never know. This could be their version of foreplay. Whatever, I was in no mood to watch.

"Obviously you two need to chat," I said, smiling like a bored therapist. I headed for the restaurant.

"No. You stay right here," commanded Dagmar.

"That's right. You're not going anywhere, buddy." At least they agreed on that.

I turned, looking first at Dagmar and then the cop. "Why

don't you two just get a camera and I'll watch the video later," I said, heading for the warmth of Myta's.

"Hey!" Shpak shouted in a loud command to freeze. I found it extremely annoying.

When I turned to face Shpak this time, I took a step towards him. Dagmar started to say something. I told her to shut the fuck up, startling her into doing just that.

"Don't be shouting at me, pal," I said. "You want to play the cop then arrest me. Otherwise why don't you shove that badge and gun up your ass."

"Frank." Dagmar spoke in the way you might say "Oh oh," and I knew I had just taken a bite of something I might not be able to chew. Still, I'd give it a good gumming if I had to. I had had enough.

"I love tough guys," Shpak said in a way that convinced me he really meant it. I noticed, however, that he was still leaning on the roof of the car. He looked unsteady, like a drunk. I decided to push a little.

"Bet you love them even more when you have help." I was referring to his late sidekick. His eyes narrowed. This would be the time. I got ready but he just stood there. He shook his head as if to clear it. Perhaps he was only saying no to himself.

"Tonight you're a lucky tough guy," he said, before sliding off the roof and down the side of the car to collapse in the street.

"Roger!" Dagmar hollered. Ever the name-caller.

She held back while I walked around the car. Shpak, crumpled and heap-like, was lying with his head propped against the rear tire. I bent down to take a closer look. His eyelids fluttered rapidly and his eyeballs showed white as they tried to climb up into his skull. I could smell booze. Even in this state his hand shot out, too fast for me, and grabbed my arm. He tried to blink into focus. His strength was gone, though, and I twisted my wrist from his already slackening fingers.

"Maybe another time, pal," I said quietly.

"Oh, my. Oh, my," he said before falling down a deep, dark well.

His breathing was shallow and irregular. I straightened him out and laid his head on the pavement. Dagmar stood behind me, miraculously silent, staring down at Shpak.

"What's going on out here?" demanded an imperious voice in a snotty, nasal tone. "I have customers, you know." It was Victoria calling out from the entrance of her daughter's restaurant.

"Must have been the garlic purée," I said, "better call 911."

"I beg your pardon," she said, coming closer to inspect. "Oh, it's you. I might have known. What's going on, Frank? I thought we'd seen the last of you."

"We need an ambulance, Victoria. No shit."

"Really," she sighed, "Then you had better call one." I followed her inside, leaving Dagmar with Shpak.

To my surprise, Dagmar insisted on riding in the ambulance. She was determined and appeared to be distracted as well.

"Who is Roman?" I asked, while they were loading Shpak into the back.

"His partner."

"Kuyek?"

"Yes."

"What did you do to him?" I asked softly.

"What? How fucking dare you!"

Two cops arrived as the ambulance pulled out. One took Shpak's ghost car. The other one asked some questions and took my name and address.

"It's lucky you happened by when you did, Mr. Weilander," said the cop.

"Call me Larry," I said, and agreed that, yes, it was fortunate.

"And this is where you can be reached?" Showing me what he had written.

"Oh yes, and anyway, I'm in the book. But like I said,

the lady in the ambulance can tell you more about it. I was just walking by."

"Okay, sir, and thanks again."

"Glad to be of help, Officer."

It had slipped out before I could see the harm. Perhaps they wouldn't connect the dots and realize that their Good Samaritan, Mr. Weilander, lived in the block next to where Shpak's partner was also hauled away. Hopefully, I'd be long gone by then.

Myta's smelled terrific, as always. It is the one unfailing test of a good restaurant. At that point I was so hungry I would have been happy with a Big Mike, so foodwise I was in the bonus round. I stood by the entrance waiting to be shown to a table. Victoria ignored me for as long as she could.

"Did the authorities not arrive yet?" she asked, finally acknowledging my presence. As if she hadn't been peeking through the curtains to soak up every detail.

"I thought I'd stay for a bite," I said, adding, "to compensate."

"Compensate for what?"

"You didn't see them? I'm surprised."

"What are you talking about? See whom?"

"The walk-in four that kept going when they saw the ambulance." I lied.

You have to be in the business to appreciate how truly irritating that can be, particularly when noticed and reported on by a peer. It's like the nosy next-door neighbour informing you smugly that your child has head lice.

"Just kidding, Victoria," I said, to help alleviate her symptoms of a red face and bulging eyes.

"Are you? How droll," she said with undisguised distaste. Who says "droll" anymore?

Nevertheless, based on the principle that you never turn business away, no matter how annoying, the busboy was summoned to show me to as remote a table as possible. It was a deuce in the far corner, away from the window and very close to the swinging door that led to the kitchen; as luck would have it, my favourite spot.

I was a bit edgy until I ate. After which, I sat back, ordered a latte and proceeded to think about what a hassle of a day it had been. Victoria kept her distance. The waiters fussed over the folks who were actually drinking, and therefore liable to give a bigger tip. Now I could relax and listen to the soothing clinks, clanks, hisses and muted voices of the kitchen serenade. Peace at last, and some time to think.

Shpak had obviously been hoist by his own petard, but how? He could die twice for all I care. As for Kuyek, I couldn't give a damn if he choked to death on kielbossa, or was smothered by a troupe of circus midgets. Too bad about Janey, and all those dogs, but what does any of it have to do with me? It's fucking madness. I don't care about any of it. Dagmar wants something or she wouldn't be keeping in touch. When did I ever hear from her or her son when they weren't after something?

Come right down to it, Donald should marry Ananah. He deserves her. My life isn't here anymore so why should I give a shit? It's obvious: paternity or no, I don't have a son. Or, if I do, fatherhood only leads to being a target for emotional abuse. And I'm not into being abused. Is any of this worth getting worked up about, worth being rousted by cops, worth getting shot at, worth supplying a few old friends and one turncoat some harmless herb? How long before the others turn on me to save their sorry asses? If I wanted that, I could have just kept my old accountant.

Be it resolved: I am now changing occupations. This instant. Trudy is just the tip of the iceberg.

The biggest thing on my mind right now, what I'm not dealing with, why I'm even allowing brain space for this shit — because all I have to do is get on a plane to make it go away — is how can I be terminal when, all things considered, I feel pretty damned good? And what's so urgent that the clinic had to call me here? Hey, how did they know where to call unless Lynnmarie told them? Would she?

I thought it was over. You reach a certain point in a relationship, where all the warts are exposed, and a delicate balance is required if you are to continue. There is usually no shortage of provocations, on either side, especially after nine years. "That's fucking it!" she said, having had enough of the three Ds: Donald, Dagmar and Dealing. Why should she care?

"'Scuse me, sir," said the waiter. I looked up and recognized him. He no longer had pink hair, and had obviously been promoted from the kitchen. "Ray wants you to call him right away at Wye ... um..."

"Weilander's?"

"Yes. He's upset." I could tell that waiter guy was upset because Ray was.

This is highly unusual, as Spock would say. Ray likes telephones even less than I do. For him to be proactive like this indicates a serious concern on his part. Ray prefers not to be serious. He thinks seriousness is a condition like its phonetic cousin, psoriasis: treatable, but difficult to get rid of, something to be avoided if at all possible. I called him. The phone rang once.

"Hello."

"Raymond, what's up?"

"I get so attached to them. That's why I don't have one," he said.

"You're talking about Gandhi?"

"Yass."

"Is he okay?"

"So far."

"Then what's the problem?" I reminded myself not to be exasperated, but I could feel it rising.

"That girl's friend, the one Gandhi didn't like."

"Cousin Omar?"

"Yass." He paused and then said, "Her, too."

"Ananah?"

"Yass."

"What did they do, Ray?" I was no longer feeling impatient. Ray was in a desperate struggle with the unfamiliar. I could hear him fight back the tremor in his voice. I had seen him like this once before and it was imperative to soothe him. Fear was only the first stage: and that stage had a short duration. I had to calm him down until I could get to him. Hopefully I could prevent what might happen next. Otherwise there would be a serious, yes, *serious*, cosmic misalignment. The atom was about to split.

Ray was getting angry.

"If it was just me, I wouldn't mind."

"C'mon, Ray, give me a hint. I'm on my way but just tell me a little. And take it slow."

"Okaay." And he took a deep breath. "They came here looking for Weilander. I only opened the door a little because Gandhi was really growling." He stopped as if he couldn't go on. Choked up a bit.

"Did they come in?"

"Heavens no. Ha. Gandhi really tried to get at them. He was trying to squeeze through the door. I could barely hold it closed. So they left."

"And that's the problem, you think they're coming back?"

"Oh yass. And he's going to shoot Gandhi."

"He said that?"

"He was talking to her. He said, 'That's the crippled bitch's dog. I thought I killed the fucker.' Then he said he was going to get a gun and come back." Ray ended on a slight quaver.

"Take it easy, Ray, he's probably bluffing." But I realized what we were dealing with.

"I don't think so."

"Ray, go to the car where we left it. I'll meet you there. Give me fifteen minutes."

"Okaay."

"And Ray..."

"Yass?"

"Go out the back and take the alley."

"Okaay."

"And before you go I want you to write a note to Weilander." I was thinking on my feet, but it should work.

"But Weilander is at Lenore's. Or are we going for a long time?" he asked hopefully.

"Just write it, Ray, and when you're finished stick it outside on the door in plain sight."

"But..."

"Ray."

"Okaay."

"Here's what I want you to say." And I dictated the note.

"Now I get it," said Ray when I was finished.

I called for a cab, ignoring Victoria's, "We should put in a line just for you." Instead I put a dollar beside the phone — which reminded me of the old lady at the Q. They were both probably from the same small town.

"Victoria, do you realize how close you are to embracing Jesus?" I asked. She took one step back, eyeballing me with some concern.

The cab crept around the corner as soon as I stepped outside. It couldn't have been the one I called, not at that speed. It lurched to a halt in front of the restaurant. The rear door flew open before I could reach for it.

"Jesus fucking Christ, could you drive any slower?" said a piqued Dagmar to the cabbie. "Frank, I'm so glad you waited," she said to me in a more honeyed tone. Then she thrust some money at the driver.

"Hey, lady, no tip is one thing, but I still need another buck for the fare."

"That's because you drove like a fucking snail," she said, as if that were the end of the debate.

I leaned into the cab. "Hang on, pal, I'll make it up to you. Gimme a sec."

"Sure thing, Boss."

"Frank," said Dagmar, in a pay-attention-to-me-not-the-help kind of voice. "Aren't you going to eat? Where are you going?"

"I already ate. Gotta go."

"You bastard. I was looking forward to this."

"How's Shpak?" I asked, reminding her that there were issues other than her plans for dinner.

"He'll probably live." Now it was my turn to be disappointed. I got in the cab.

"Frank, I need to talk to you. I want you to help me find something."

"Tomorrow, maybe."

"No. Tomorrow will be too late. Tonight!"

"Stay away from the ragoût of Guinea fowl. If you ask me, it's a few noodles shy of even being chicken soup." And the cab took off as if on cue.

"Frank!" she hollered.

I'll say this for Dagmar — and Donald, too: when they want something they really go after it. And they don't mind stamping their feet, holding their breath and turning a little blue to get it.

"Nice going, Boss. But then you could always handle the women."

"J.O.E. Joe," I said. "How the hell are you?"

That's the thing about a small city, the heaven and hell of it. You can't hide because everyone knows who you are. You can't embrace, exchange numbers, be vague about your activities and never see one another again after promising to keep in touch. The best you can manage is, in mid-winter, when everybody has cabin fever, to mutually cross to the other side of the street to avoid having to speak to one another.

With J.O.E. Joe you wouldn't have to cross the street. He worked part time at the restaurant during his student days. Easy going, dependable, principled, humorous and sympathetic, he is the kind of person that makes you long for home sometimes. He teased me about his Bruins, who were on the ascendency, and my Canadiens, who seemed to be headed backwards towards oblivion, all the way to the cathedral's parking lot.

He refused my money for the ride. "That's okay, Boss. I didn't even have the meter on."

Ray and Gandhi materialized from behind a lilac bush at the edge of the lot. At first I didn't see the dog. The telltale patch of white bandage was gone. Was the note in place? Yes it was. Did it direct the reader to meet at the intersection instead of halfway down the block where we would be hidden? Yes it did. Perfect. Wait. Was the note written in longhand or printed in block letters? This was the one thing I hadn't stressed. Ray's handwriting was as unfettered as his approach to personal hygiene. You practically needed a degree in Egyptology to figure it out.

"I printed," said Ray, pleased with himself. Coming out of his funk.

"So is Gandhi healed, Ray, or has he just decided to abandon the turban and assimilate?" I asked as we drove off to my storage locker.

"The bandage really sticks out at night. If he gets infected we can fix it later. If he gets shot ..."

"He won't get hurt, Ray. We'll take good care of him." I hoped that were true. "At least we know who took those shots at us."

"We do?"

"Well, don't you think?"

"I missed it earlier," Ray said thoughtfully. "There was a bump and some swelling just beside the wound, consistent with a blow from a heavy object. It wasn't from the shot."

"Meaning what?"

"I really couldn't say except I think Gandhi has met this person before."

I left it at that. The math was all there, it just needed summing up. Hopefully my note would lure Omar close enough to get at him. If he showed up with a .243 I could rest my case, even if it couldn't be proven in court. Not that

I had the slightest intention of letting it get that far.

We parked at the south end of the weedy vacant lot, about seventy-five feet away from the building on the north side that housed the storage space. The intersection identified in Ray's note was further north still. To reach my car from there you would first have to pass my space and then the vacant lot. I persuaded Ray that Gandhi would be safer in the car. We left the doors unlocked as a compromise.

I should kick my ass for not paying attention, for letting my focus waver, but who is to say that things would have turned out differently? Ray appeared to be deep in thought, which was disconcerting in and of itself and I let that distract me.

We creaked along a wooden-planked corridor that was lit dimly by a high window. Lumens spilled in from the streetlight. I unlocked the locker door, which opened outward like the one at the entrance, and ushered Ray inside. After I had closed up and twisted the deadbolt, I flipped the switch and the desk lamp came on. I had no secrets from Ray, not here anyway, so I went directly to the false panel and showed him how it worked. I took out the grass and sat Ray down to roll us a joint. Mostly, it was to keep him busy while I assembled the shotgun.

"Just put the stuff back and close it like I showed you when you're finished."

"Okaay," he said, somewhat cheerier.

It took all of thirty seconds to put the gun together and stick the box back on the shelf. Then I took a five-pack of slugs and a handful of the heavier shot and put them in opposite pockets of my jacket. Finally, with the safety on, I loaded one shell in the breech and two in the magazine. All set, I realized, but for one small detail.

It's called a trigger lock. Cost me twelve ninety-five at the hardware store. It sits inside the trigger guard, occupying the entire space and enveloping the trigger. You can load the gun, cock it, release the safety and it still cannot be fired. You need to pull the trigger for that, which you can't do when the trigger lock is in place. It makes the gun safe from children and strangers, and it can be unlocked with a small key. Like the one in my suitcase in the trunk of the car. Swell.

The irony is not lost on me. Using a trigger lock is one of several safety practices I follow religiously. Years of ingrained good habits have fixed it so that, if you went hunting with me, the last thing that would happen to you would be to be shot by my gun. Unless I wanted to. Everything I do in the field stresses keeping the muzzle from ever pointing in your direction. Now that I may need to use my gun against a person all that works against me. I would never have forgotten that key if I was on my way to bang some ducks.

"Tell me, Ray, is lock-picking one of your hidden talents, hitherto unknown to your associates?"

"Um, not really, no."

"Then I have to go to the car and retrieve a key."

"Oh oh."

"It'll be okay. Douse the light until I leave and lock the door behind me."

"Okaay." He sounded so distracted that I went over to the desk. There were several crumpled cigarette papers lying about, including one stuck to his thumbnail that he was trying to flick off. Grass spilled out everywhere.

"I'm doing something wrong, aren't I?"

"Criminal, in fact."

"No, I mean the rolling part," he said.

"So do I."

"Ha. It's been so long. I thought I was doing it right."

"Try licking the gluey part after you get it rolled," I advised.

"Whoopsy."

"Ray?"

"Yass."

"I'm going now. When I come back I'll knock three times before I unlock the door. Turn out the light when you hear me knock. If you hear a key in the lock without three knocks you have a problem."

"I don't like the sound of this," Ray said, shaking his head.

"Okay, three whistles then." It was an attempt that fizzled. "The light, Ray."

"Okaay." And click, it went black.

Softly I walked to the entrance, pausing every few steps to listen and to give my eyes a chance to adjust to the dark. It was just a precaution. There should be plenty of time. I waited just inside the outer door an extra long time before stepping outside. Omar stood on the sidewalk, grinning.

"How about having one on me?" he said, waving the mickey of Scotch I had given him. It held about half the amount I had left in it. I realized then that what Shpak was trying to say was "Omar" — not "oh my".

"Thanks just the same, but I'm trying to give it up." And I tried to walk past him to my car.

"That so?" he said, and casually punched me in the solar plexus.

chapter fifteen

It was an awkward moment. Whether Omar saw it as a successful sortie of the non-verbal kind, or I viewed it as a failed attempt to convey one's thoughts verbally, became instantly moot. It was a communication issue and the medium was indeed the message.

In most of your common, garden-variety scraps there is fear going in but, barring a shot to one of the vital areas, relatively little pain during the encounter. The tussle of normal fisticuffs is far more affecting on the mind. It can eat at you, win or lose, for months or years afterwards, every move replayed endlessly in your head. If you are the winner you could have won bigger, more decisively. You're almost better off losing — except for the nagging couldas, shouldas, and what ifs.

The threat of violence is usually enough. In most conflicted situations there is a lot more bluster and bluff than hand-to-hand combat. Even in mating ruts there appears to be more posturing than actual locking of horns. But every now and again some young buck, inflamed with lust, is going to take the hard road and do more than just rattle his antlers. He will have to be more than evenly matched to win. It will take a large measure of agility and strength, an extra helping, way beyond a little bit better. He is fighting experience, wiles, tradition and mental dominance.

When Omar hit me I went down.

It hurt — the searing pain of the hot poker. Electric. Sudden. Piercing. Immediate. It hurt when I couldn't breathe, gasping like a lonesome cod in an empty hold. It hurt worse when breathing resumed.

A younger, taller animal had cut through the wiles. Clearly he had more experience, having been knocked about and doing considerable knocking of his own in a never-ending quest to even the score. Physically he was so much the superior being we didn't even talk the same language in matters pugnacious. He was skinny, like this kid I knew who was beaten daily by a succession of dads since before he could talk. You had to pity anyone who got into a scrap with that scrawny little bastard. You could hit him a thousand times and never stop his relentless pursuit. His bones thickened, although he stayed thin, and by the time he dropped out of high school even the mega-jocks breathed a thankful prayer. Omar appeared to be of that ilk.

In the natural world once you're down that's it. You've lost. It isn't like pro boxing, where you can survive a knockdown in the early rounds to bob and weave your way to a split decision. There is no referee, no standing eight count, and no weight categories in the alley. There are no rules but one: once you go down you're dinner.

When I went down I landed flat on my ass and then doubled over. I was wide open for whatever came next: a kick to the head, a stomp on my right hand that was holding me up, or another boot to the solar plexus which would break the fingers of my left hand as it probed the damage. There was nothing I could do except await the coup de grace.

I was outraged. I was fucked.

What saved me, at least in the short term, was my inability to interpret this non-verbal communiqué. Had I known what was on his mind, I might have moved instead of sitting there. Our views differed when it came to dominance and subjugation. The bull paws the ground before he charges, whereas with the bear it could merely be a bluff. Aggression is wonderfully direct. It also creates its own momentum. Omar's rules not only include aggression but embrace it. With him and his fellows, body language is a version of ESP. Mine told him all was as it should be.

So he didn't follow up the first blow. I'm sitting there loathing my position and he didn't take another shot. He only needed the first punch to establish dominance. It was done quickly, with a minimum of effort. The way I fell, my surprise, the way I just sat there while the pain resonated in perfect waves, the fact that he had not hit me particularly hard by his reckoning, indicated to him the success of his endeavour. All was well. The next phase could begin.

We had once again failed to communicate. He wanted something from me — otherwise he would have finished the job — and was ready to move on. As for me, the helpless baby, I was still hopelessly mired in phase one and not prepared to embrace whatever came next. The question I asked myself was should I roll over, sit up and beg, or soldier on? The matter had already been concluded in Omar's mind. My body language told him that. So, instead of hitting me again, he casually, arrogantly reached down, grabbed my jacket, and hauled me to my feet.

It was my first attempt at head butting. I've only ever seen it done in British movies. It seems terribly effective, particularly when administered by a monosyllabic skinhead. The other guy's nose is bloodied and broken. All the fight goes out of them. You win. For most of us — think of the last time you barked your shin or stubbed your toe — pain is a command to cease, desist and tend to the wounded part. For Omar I knew it would be a stimulant, so it was imperative to double up the jab, as it were. I banged him again. The second blow landed so squarely that I nearly lost a filling. The first hadn't been too shabby either.

He was hurt to the extent that he let go of me and staggered back a step. Blood was indeed pouring from his nose. He shook his head to clear it, which was a good sign. He sneered, wiping his nose with the back of his hand, and reached behind his back. Fumbling under his jacket he finally pulled out some sort of commando knife, blackened blade and all.

I wished with all my heart that it were a gun. People don't always shoot straight, but up close most of us can stab real good. The fear in the pit of my stomach shifted farther south. I thought of all the times I've ever been cut, even by paper. Has it ever been a pleasant experience?

For some reason I thought about a hot afternoon, hunting with Weilander. We had shot some birds early and he was field dressing them so they didn't spoil. Make a knife-slit through the anus, reach up into the cavity, and pull out all the innards in a gooey red mass. Some organs came gracefully while others had to be twisted and tugged, putting up a great deal of resistance, like trying to snap a particularly thick rubber band. Weilander didn't especially enjoy this, nor was it much fun to watch. Guts were all over the place when he finished. His hand was bloody to the wrist.

The last time somebody pulled a knife on me I was twenty, quicksilver-fast, muscles of whipcord. That's how I remember it, anyway. The guy was a little bigger than Omar, meaner looking, and nowhere near as tough. I had been getting the best of him so he pulled a knife. I jumped backward and grabbed a softball sized rock. Advantage me. The guy took off and that was the end of it. Omar wasn't afraid. He was just being practical. As for me, there has been a significant deterioration of my physical abilities. The normal process of ageing. I know, at least, the scope of the damage via aching muscles and sprains that take an eon to heal. So what would a smart guy do, miles from the nearest rock? Step back. I could do that much at least.

My jacket was heavy with the shells that were zippered into the side pockets. I had to remove it to have any hope. Omar jumped at me when I got one sleeve off. Big mistake. He landed on the sleeve and when I tugged to release it he lost his balance long enough for me to free the other arm. Now I had a weapon too, a rudimentary bolas. The old sand in the sock trick. Omar smiled when I waved the jacket.

The whole time I was trying to work my way to the car and maybe get a little help from Gandhi. Ray wouldn't like it, but what was I to do? Omar sensed this and managed to keep himself between me and my vehicle. The clock was ticking. Adrenaline will only carry you so far before fatigue sets in with a vengeance. Omar, realizing this, set to lunging at me, feinting and jabbing. He was almost being playful until I corked him one on his knife hand with my weighted pocket. It hurt, not enough for him to drop the knife, but enough for him to slow down and appreciate the quality of my jacket in a way he hadn't before. Still, we both figured he could outwait me, so I had to make the move.

Despite a series of swoops and sweeps with my jacket I was losing ground. Omar had driven me past the entrance to the storage locker and was herding me up the street. It was like nearing the end of a long squash rally. I was one or two boasts from collapse. Then all Omar would have to do is catch my jacket and reel me in. Even my terror of the knife was waning. I was becoming irresolute and in grave danger when I saw the light.

Omar saw the light, too. In fact, it shone full in his face and blinded him, stopping him dead in his tracks. As he tried to shade his eyes I stepped up to the plate and nailed him in the temple with a pocketful of shot. He fell to his hands and knees. I clouted him again, roughly in the same spot. It was a good swing, lots of follow-through. He kind of toppled over sideways and went all the way down.

The knife was still in his hand until I mashed his devil tattoo with both feet and kicked it away. He was down and out, helpless. Where once I was too tired I now was frenzied with energy. I reared back and kicked him solidly in the balls. Then, to the Marquess of Queensbury's dismay, I kept on kicking him. In the face, the ribs, the balls again, anywhere I thought it would do the most harm, cause the most pain. I couldn't stop until Ray's big arms embraced me and effortlessly pulled me away.

"Time out," he chimed, giving me a hug, calming me. It felt good.

"Just doing a bit of communicating with Omar," I said, catching my breath.

"My goodness, he's not much of a talker, is he?" Ray laughed.

"Not for the moment."

The bright light went out and a body materialized out of the dark carrying a jack handle.

"Sorry I took so long, Boss, but I had to make sure I aimed it right," Joe explained and then said, "Oh, hi, Ray, how's it goin'?"

"Very well, I think," said the emperor, bowing. "How are you, Joe?"

"Can't complain, I guess," replied Joe, as if any minute now he and Ray were about expound on the state of this year's crop.

You don't see them much any more, but a few cabbies still have the 75,000-candlepower spotlights to search for house numbers. Joe, or more probably his dad, was one of them. Now that I've seen them in action, I want one too. And I wouldn't say no to a cigarette either.

"I owe you big-time, Joe. You saved my ass for sure," I said in fluent local dialect. I was dripping in sweat and still short of breath.

"Aw, don't worry about it. 'Sides, it's a slow night

ennaway. That's how come I could follow that guy when I seen him follow you."

"Saw."

"Right, Boss. Saw. When I saw him follow you. Heck, I seen he was up to no good right away," Joe amended, to his and Ray's snorts of amusement.

So much for my Judas note. Omar must have spotted us while he was on his way to Weilander's.

Ray caught me looking hard at Omar, who was lying inert and unmoving like a fallen Combat Ken doll. He bent over to take a closer look, poking and prodding cautiously. At one point he gingerly turned Omar over to check the back of his head. I took little pleasure in his swollen, battered and bloody face, but at least it wasn't me lying there.

"How's the patient, Ray?" I asked after giving him a minute.

"He's alive but he could probably use a hospital."

"Seems like the waste of a good bed." Ray said nothing, just looked at me. "But we'll do that," I added.

"Soon would be good."

"Okay, Ray, soon. By the way, I told you he was bluffing about the gun."

"I don't think so." And he turned Omar enough so that I could see a bulge in the back pocket of his pants.

I kneeled with a groan and tried to extract the gun with the sleeve of my jacket. It was caught on something which explains why he had gone for the knife instead. Finally I pried loose a small, older model, chrome .22 automatic with worn black handle grips. A strand of cotton was stuck to the front sight. I should buy a lottery ticket, I thought, as I struggled to my feet, nearly banging heads with Joe. It reminded me of the tender spot on my forehead.

"Guns, Boss. Ho-lee." Then in afterthought: "Hey, where's the other one?"

"You saw another gun?"

"No. In the car. There were two guys in the car."

"Which car, Joe?"

"That old shit bucket over there." He pointed to a rusted out K car with Ontario plates. With Omar's gun I moved towards it cautiously.

She was curled up foetally on the front seat, her head beside the steering wheel. I opened the passenger side door and she raised her head slowly, fearfully. She blinked and looked at me, then at the gun still wrapped in my sleeve, the one with Omar's prints all over it. I looked at the gun, too, and then back at her. She took her gaze off the weapon and stared at me. Her eyes narrowed momentarily, replacing the goat with a glimpse of cat. She got up to a sitting position, slid across the seat, and threw her arms around my neck, holding tight.

"Ew, Daddy, I was, like, sew scared," she said in a husky whisper.

The sour odour was gone. She didn't smell half bad, I thought. She must have had a bath. The small tingle I felt in my nether regions, a subversive stirring, must have been some sort of post-adrenal hiccup. I quickly pried her arms from around my neck.

I was about to say "Tell it to someone who cares," when she confessed.

"He's not really my cousin, yew know. I met him in Toronto and he, like, helped me out one time." She said this as if it were a question. "And he's like, I don't know, kind of a hard guy to get rid of. I didn't want to be here at all."

Point taken. She was about to say more, but I cut her off. The last thing I needed was for her to suddenly assume human dimensions. Tough to believe, for starters.

"Why don't you drive yourself home, then? Omar won't be needing the car tonight."

"Is he, like, dead or anything?"

"Not dead. The best we can hope for is that he's in a lot of pain."

"Really?"

"Really."

"Ew."

"And, Ananah?"

"Yeah?"

"I'm only going to tell you this one more time."

"What?"

"Don't call me 'Daddy.'"

"Ew, you are, like, sew funny." She appeared to be greatly amused as she slid over to the driver's seat. "Now don't forget you know what," she added, before I slammed the passenger door shut.

"You can bet your ass on that," I muttered as she drove down the street. Were it not for Ray and Joe I could have shot the bitch.

Slowly I walked back to where Omar lay. He hadn't moved. I was beginning to stiffen up. I hadn't done my post death-struggle stretch.

"I tell you, Ray, I have a real problem with that girl."

"Yass, I know."

"She's beginning to warm up to me."

"That little ingrate! And after all you've tried to do," he said.

Ray looked at me inquisitively, then pointed at Omar.

I had given it some thought, motioned for Ray to wait, and went and got my cell phone from the trunk. This time I also got the trigger lock key, not that I would be needing it. I dialled Robbie, who picked up on the first ring and asked me to wait while he took himself outside for privacy.

"We got the bastard, Frank. Shpak's prints are all over the pill container and the glass vial."

"Meaning what?"

"Stealing evidence, tampering, he's off the force at the very least."

"You know he's in the hospital?"

"I got a guy over there watching him right now. They're trying to bring him around. We'll charge him when he wakes up."

"He'll live then?"

"I'm afraid so, Frank." Robbie was pretty happy. Then his tone changed. "Got the forensics on Janey and Kuyek

... hey, wait a minute. How do you know about Shpak?"

"I was standing outside Myta's when they hauled him away."

"Oh." You could hear the gears working. "I wondered why Weilander was out when he should have been holed up." Then he laughed, "I'd love to know what you're really up to."

"I'm just trying to survive, old friend. What about Janey and Kuyek?"

"She was smothered. Somebody drugged her and then put a pillow over her face." His voice was grim. "Apparently she had a dog, too, one of those companion dogs. It's gone missing."

"A female Rottweiler," I said. Ray's head swivelled towards me. I waved him off.

Robbie went silent, then chose his words carefully.

"Don't tell me you know anything about this, Frank. Or Ray."

"Well, I think I know something, Robbie. I just found out. But that's just the trouble isn't it?"

"What?"

"With your profession. Sooner or later we're all suspects."

"No, Frank. Just the people who seem to have inside knowledge of unsolved crimes."

"How about I send you the guy who likely smothered her, does that get me and Ray off the hook?"

"Can you do that?"

"Yep. Except you'll have to pay the cab fare and you'll have to wait until he wakes up to talk to him."

Robbie was happy again and amazed when I told him what I had discovered. The stuff I left out wasn't important. We worked out a way to keep me out of it. For now, at least.

"Joe is going to be driving on Dewdney East when he spots this guy lying on the sidewalk. He drags him to the cab, sees the knife and gun and drives to you instead of the hospital. He really doesn't know what this is all about anyway. Okay?"

"Okay," Robbie confirmed.

"Ray says he'll testify as to hearing Omar talk about the dog. Ananah probably will, too, if she thinks it will keep her ass out of trouble."

"Jesus, Frank. You'd make a good cop."

"Fuck off."

"We got another problem with Kuyek, though." Robbie was still laughing. It's been a long time since I'd heard him so happy.

"What?" I snapped, still annoyed by his insult.

"He did choke to death, but there was enough poison in that sausage to kill three guys. The same stuff that's being used on all those dogs."

"Any bite marks on Kuyek?"

"No. Why?"

"Must have been a small dog he beat up for that kielbossa then. Fuck, do I have to do all your work for you?"

Robbie was roaring with laughter when I hung up. Ray, however, was not as relaxed as he might have been.

"We could injure him further if we just dump him in the cab," he said.

"In what way?" I asked, looking for pointers.

"Well," said Ray, pausing to ponder. "I don't think I should tell you."

"That's okay, Ray, Joe and I can figure it out by ourselves. I'm thinking drop him in the back sideways on the floor, Joe."

"Sounds good to me, Boss."

"I'd rather tie him to the bumper and drag him there," I said, just to get the point across to Ray that at least we were getting the prick some help.

"I think I'll check on Gandhi," was his response.

Joe went to his cab to open the back door and to get the supermarket bag I told him we needed. I rifled Omar's pockets. When Joe came back I put the knife and gun carefully into the Superstore bag. Then we each took an arm, dragged Omar to the cab and dumped him in the back as planned. He weighed a ton, dead weight. I experienced a sense of déjà vu as we wrestled with our load, but it wasn't about Ananah. It was like an archetypal memory: wheeling a cart through cobbled streets and stopping to pile on another plague-ridden body. Joe's face took on a Breughelian cast under the street lights. Same tribe.

"Sorry about all the hassle, Joe," I said, handing him two hundred-dollar bills — US dollars. He took the money, having seen me remove it from Omar's wallet. He placed the weapons in the front seat.

"S'okay, Boss. It's been kinda dull around here lately." I gave him the thumbs up as he drove off.

Not that it would have mattered, but I'm reasonably sure he hadn't seen me retrieve the larger wad of cash from the inside pocket of Omar's jacket. He did note my snort of amusement when I checked Omar's ID, but said nothing. Robbie was going to have an even bigger laugh.

Ray had the rear door of the car open. He and Gandhi were crooning away to one another in the back seat. Lots of doggie this and doggums that mixed with delirious licking sounds. A couple of crazy kids in love.

"I gotta lock up, Ray, and then we'll go."

"Okaay."

Judging by the debris, it had taken a half dozen cigarette papers for Ray to get it right. It was an acceptable joint, although somewhat funnel shaped. I cleaned up and put everything away. There was almost eight thousand dollars in US hundreds and fifties in the roll of cash. I put that with the roofies, though I was beginning to wish they were painkillers. Tomorrow, especially, I was going to need some. Maybe even tonight. I sat on the folding metal chair.

All the peripheral stuff was out of the way. Gone as suddenly as it had appeared. It had been like doing a walk-on at the end of the third act in a tragic farce. Shpak won't be showing up on my doorstep. Kuyek won't be showing up on anybody's doorstep. Omar would likely be gone for a long time. He wouldn't be breaking Donald's bones any more, which is what I figured had happened that time he showed up in a cast. For sure I worked off some karma with that.

Now I had time to refocus on job one. Why did I feel so gloomy? Maybe the fatigue. I'm tired. So the first thing to do is get some sleep.

"Let's go back to Weilander's, Ray," I said, back at the car. "I'm beat."

"The excitement seems to have whetted Gandhi's appetite."

"You can tell?"

"Oh yass."

"We can stop for pizza then. But let's hurry. I need some rest. I have a call to make in the morning."

"What was that you put in the trunk?"

"My shotgun."

"Oh."

"Relax. It's just for comfort, Ray. Just for comfort."

chapter sixteen

All I had to go on, really, were fish. I'm thinking of the sleek trout in the Kettle River, and one particular day. Poole was in the stern of an old wood-lined green canvas canoe. He was paddling while I fished. A few days earlier we had dropped acid up on the Weed farm, a saddle of pasture and bunch grass that sat high above the valley on a toothless ridge. Tame stuff, mountainwise, although we were high enough to look south, way down into Washington state, across the rounded backs and lesser humps of the Kettle Range. Far below we could see the thin silver glint of the river as it wound around rocky outcrops and meandered a tree-lined course through the valley.

It had gone well. I had managed to stay centred while the banshees and demons of daily life howled through my mind like a paisley tornado, gathering intensity until they exploded in a crystal starburst, flooding the world with a clear white light. You have to die to be reborn.

Clean. In the resolution phase, the settling, the glorious sense of totality that rebirth brings, of being one with the cosmos and all living things, and part of the One, feeling the oneness, the not separateness. The goal is won, the grail sought and found.

With my eyes shut I see the mauves and purples of a

twilight inhabited by tall, conical, snow-topped peaks; perhaps the Andes. A figure descends a well-worn trail. It is an old man astride a donkey, his sandalled feet nearly touching the ground. His thick hair and neatly trimmed beard are white. His rough cotton peasant's shirt and drawstring trousers are white. But his poncho is rainbow-striped and radiant, reflecting the colours of sky and rock in streams of warmth and vitality. Atop his head, at a jaunty angle, is a battered straw cowboy hat with a low, flat crown.

Slowly, surely, he moves along a path parallel to my own. When he is opposite to where I stand he turns to me. He smiles and waves. I am absorbed into his eyes, golden with the sure love of belonging. I know him and have always known him. I wave back as he passes and continues along the trail, ascending the ever-diminishing ribbon, that leads to an even higher peak. His smile and mine remain with me, warming me as night steals in. It is Poole.

"You saw the Old Man," he says, when I tell him I had seen him in a vision. "He's an archetype. I see him too sometimes. When I'm lucky." He paddled around a sweep into safer water as he spoke; returning the vision and its power to its source, to reside within me, where it belongs.

The benign sense of promise is sharpened and brought instantly into focus by the shock of a fish hitting your line. A small drama unfolds. It is not always certain you will land the trout. It's not a done deal until you have it in your hands. Hold fast even then.

I have a silvery, fat rainbow clutched firmly in my left hand. I remove the hook, brutishly, as the barbs tear through its cheek. There must be no more suffering. I reach for the short hardwood stick and deftly clout it on the head. In the many times I have repeated this act there is a moment I have become used to, mysterious though it be. The fish is alive, a coiled muscle, until the cosh descends. Then, whumpf, life is gone, just like that. There is a definable jolt, electric. I feel it every time. A tiny, curious sensation, a small current of energy is released at the instant of death. Lao Tzu says: "Its quickness is its quietness again."

What was let go? Where did it go? Since one is all and all is one, into what form did it transmute? And what does it animate, since the world appears no less diminished?

Poole is gone now. He is dead. Both he and the day's trout, however, live within me still.

I was prepared to kill birds, or so I thought. Weilander started me out on ruffed grouse.

"They're the easiest, eh."

The ravines that cut into the sides of the flat plain and tumble at varying pitches down to the aged valley floor are lush clefts of bush and trees. They are called coulees. Like bluffs, which is what prairie folk call the stands of trees and bush that dot the middle and edges of grainfields like emerald islands in a golden lake, they have an abundant concentration of wildlife.

We started down the coulee late, having been sidetracked by the flock of chicken we chased for an hour or so without getting a shot off. Weilander could never ignore a congregation of sharptails, no matter what. It's like waving a flock of sheep at a border collie. He made up for the fruitless chase by banging four ruffies within a half hour, the last two of which he had politely pointed out to me first. I couldn't spot them and he shot away. "Okay, the next one is yours, but shoot, for fucksakes." It was getting dark. "Right," I said, feeling vaguely silly.

"Evening is the best time of day," he was saying as we laboured back uphill. "They move up the coulee to catch the last rays. Lotsa times they'll be sitting up in the trees on top. If you see that, shoot the bottom one. The others might still sit. Shoot the top guy and they'll all flush."

"Okay," I said, gripping my brand new Wingmaster tighter.

We were prowling carefully, about twenty feet apart, when I saw my bird. I stopped a bit too abruptly, raised my gun a little too quickly, and shot a tad hurriedly. Still, I nailed it just as it was taking wing. It flopped around in the brush.

"Nice shot," said Weilander. "But you better get on it quick."

I crashed through the bush like a charging rhino, on the bird in a flash. Now what? Right away I knew this was not like fishing. I grabbed for the bird and got a wing that fluttered itself out of my grasp. I was the comic relief in a nature movie until I got one hand around the grouse's legs. Then I put my shotgun down.

Next, of course, I had to finish the job of killing. There was no stick at hand to administer the final blow. So, thinking laterally, I took the bird by the legs, one in each hand, and moved over to a Manitoba maple. The plan was to hit the stick with the bird, to brain the hapless creature against the slender tree trunk. I took aim and swung it like a baseball bat, once, twice, three times. Each time I did this the poor grouse would pull his head up and out of the way. His eyes, which had a worried look, stared at me. They bored into me, as real as a pigeon in the park. There was a Disney cartoon aspect to this, of Alice and her flamingo mallet, but it was not a fun moment.

"Let me show you something," said Weilander, reaching for the bird to my great relief.

I offered no resistance as he grasped the grouse's neck as tightly as you would a lasso. He swung its body around in circles to break its neck. This clearly wasn't like killing fish. Fish live in water. Their eyes don't see as ours do, as a bird's can. They struggle but they don't see you. They don't look in your eyes. They don't implore.

Once I got past that, I developed a great love for the hunt. I couldn't wait for the summer to end — not that I minded the blind faith of fishing. I learned to read a coulee, or the edge of a field, or a stand of natural habitat butting up against a field of wheat, as readily as a fly fisherman can interpret the back eddies and deep pools in a stream. I can see the tall grass sway, or watch leaves tremble, and tell you if it's the wind or a creature. But I have never felt that moment with birds, when the life drains out of them.

I swing them around as I was taught, then fold their necks around my thumb, choking them to make sure. I hold them like that for a long time. Occasionally, I would let go too soon and they'd still be alive, gasping through their broken neck. I'd have to fold and repeat, holding them far longer than was necessary, my teeth clenched the entire time.

Ray finally appeared from the side door of Georgie's carrying two large flat boxes. The window had to be lowered on the trip to Weilander's. The aromatic combination of hot pizza, dog, and a sweaty Ray was teetering on the cusp between riotous stench and something vaguely erotic. Neither was acceptable. I just wanted to get there, so I drove directly, incautiously, to the house and parked in front. Weilander's half-ton was gone. The only other car on the street was an Antelope cab parked down the block at the edge of the turning circle. Hardly any independents left; it's all Antelope now, I thought, even Joe.

"You two go in and set up, Ray. I'm going to get a few things from the trunk."

"Okaay, but hurry. I don't think Gandhi can wait very long."

Gandhi, in fact, began to growl with a certain degree of menace, looking right at me.

"Looks like he doesn't want to share, either," I said.

"Now, now. Where are your manners, boy?" Ray said as he herded Gandhi into the house. I watched them enter and was about to open the trunk when a shadowy figure rose from behind a hedge across the street. He walked stiffly towards me. His face was puffed up, purple and blood-caked. In his left hand he held a small gun: it was pointed at my stomach. His right hand dangled uselessly, but you could still make out the tattoo.

"You wouldn't last very long inside, pal. You kick like a girl," Omar sneered.

"How about you put the gun away and I'll see if I can do any better."

"I'm going to do you slow and watch. First I want my fucking money."

"What money?"

"You think I was out when you rifled my pockets? Give."

"I don't have it."

"Okay," he said and took a step closer, getting ready to shoot.

"You're going to shoot me anyway," I said, giving him a big smile. "At least this way you don't get the money." That slowed him down.

The idea was to get the car between him and me. The .22 wasn't very powerful, not powerful enough to go through two car windows and still do damage, but I didn't want to find out how good a shot he was left-handed if it could be avoided. On the whole, though, I was liking this a lot better than the knife.

"We'll see. I'll fucking even us up anyway." And he aimed for my leg and pulled the trigger in one quick motion, too fast for me to react.

Nothing happened. He pulled the trigger again, not even aiming, and still nothing.

It used to happen quite often during the early years. The prospect of being skunked looms large as you trudge up the last coulee. When you finally see a bird everything is fluid as you take your stance, raise the gun smoothly, take aim and pull the trigger. Except it doesn't budge, it is rigid, no give whatsoever. It's like squeezing a quarter in the crook of your finger. The only thing that happens is that the harder you squeeze the more it hurts. And every time, not just the first time or the first few times, it takes a couple of seconds to figure out what's happening — let alone react. By the time you release the safety the bird is long gone. It makes no sense to shoot at this point, but quite often you do in a wasted, futile gesture, sending the lead shot howling through the air.

I took two strides and ripped the gun from Omar's fingers, hurting him in the process. The move appeared so practiced it looked like I had been doing it for years. Step, step, grip, snap, groan, you're fucked. The point is I had clearly had enough, weary of wasting time on these lowlifes. Without even trying I was buried in other people's shit. Other people? No. Not other people. Dag-fucking-mar and Donald. Their shit. When did they have to deal with my shit? Never.

Well, all that could change in a hurry.

Donald, even as a child, couldn't stand being alone for more than two minutes. He didn't know how to spend time by himself. To someone like me, who needs long periods of solitude to maintain any sort of equilibrium, this was a mystery. By the time he reached adolescence and was living with me it had gotten right out of hand. You couldn't so much as take a shit without having to talk to him through the bathroom door.

Donald had some friends — good friends, who were intelligent, lively and loyal, who were attracted by his charisma. Eventually they would have to go home to supper, or practice sports, or do homework; exercising some of the disciplines. This left a vacuum that was only too readily filled by the bottom edge of the companionship spectrum; they besieged the house with phone calls while the world ate supper, or tried to.

The concept of discrimination has taken a bad rap. You must be able to discriminate. If you can't tell the difference between a sausage and a lump of shit, mealtime is going to be fraught with peril; especially if you drag little Omar home and ask can he stay for dinner.

Full-grown Omar was cursing me while he held his left hand between his ribs and right bicep. At least he wasn't whining. I resisted giving him another boot in the nuts, asking him how girlish he felt that one was. Instead I solidly connected with his kneecap. He used both hands to break his fall. My inner sadist was delighted by his reaction, but all I was doing was keeping him in one place. I had no fear of Omar. Having beaten him once I could beat him a thousand times.

He watched as I cocked the little gun. A shell ejected, and I caught it in mid-air with some panache. I flicked the safety, something that had escaped him. It was ready.

"What happened to Joe?" I asked quietly, almost gently.

"Who the fuck is Joe?"

"You're driving his cab."

"He's keeping my knife warm, asshole."

How sad that was to hear. How very, very sad.

"Too bad for Joe and too bad for you," I said, as I swung the gun towards him and pulled the trigger two feet from his head. Splat. The bullet hit the pavement and ricocheted into the night. Omar had moved as quickly as you might expect. He had the reflexes of a terrified grouse. I raised the gun again.

"Wait!" There was something akin to respect in his voice. It was only fear, but it would do. He had misjudged me, badly. "He's not hurt. He got the knife and I got the gun. He ran off."

Ray opened the door and peered out. "Is everything okay?" He struggled to hold Gandhi.

"Yes, Ray." The moment had passed. I slid the clip out of the gun and tossed the automatic onto Weilander's lawn where I could retrieve it later when I had resumed a more cosmic perspective. The clip went into my pocket.

"Here comes the police," Ray said. I looked up to see a cruiser glide slowly down the block and stop in the middle of the street. This would save me a call to Robbie, I thought, before the door opened and Shpak got out. He held a gun that was a lot bigger than the one I had just thrown away. A testament to the wonders of modern medicine, Shpak looked at me and grinned. He glanced sideways at Omar and shook his head. Ray ducked back inside.

"Nice work, Tough Guy. Save me the trouble of kicking his ass." To Omar he said, "Get up you little fucker. I'll show you what happens to guys that try to take me out, brother or no brother."

"What are you talking about?" Omar struggled painfully to his feet.

"Like you didn't try to do me with that doped Scotch," Shpak snorted.

"What? I didn't put anything in that until an hour ago, after you had a shot. I tried to give some to Daddy here. It was his Scotch in the first place. He gave it to me." Omar looked at me thoughtfully.

"That's right," said a muffled voice from the front seat of the cruiser.

"I told you to shut up," Shpak said to the voice. "Get out here. No, this side." Ananah slid across the seat and out the door. She stood uncertainly beside Shpak.

"Is that right, Tough Guy?"

I just shrugged.

"Ew, Daddy." Ananah looked at me the way Omar had, but she didn't get a chance to voice her next thought. Shpak grabbed her by the shoulder and shook her violently.

"Shut the fuck up, you stupid bitch."

I could see that Dagmar was not the only area of commonality between me and Shpak. Still, I almost felt for the little goat when she gasped.

"Where's the bottle now?" he asked Omar.

"I left it somewhere," Omar replied sheepishly. How could he know that this lethal, double-dosed, quarter-full pint of Scotch was currently burning a hole in the inside pocket of my jacket? I couldn't leave it for some kid to find.

"You can't do anything without fucking up, can you?"

Shpak said to his kid brother before herding us into the house. Omar said nothing. He limped around and found the .22 automatic, and then held out his mangled hand to me. I handed him the clip. He took it absently, not paying me much heed at all. I knew we'd both kill for a decent painkiller. Perhaps a bad choice of words.

Ray stood off to the side, in front of Weilander's closed bedroom door. His hands were clasped as if in prayer, resting under his chin. With his head bowed slightly forward he looked out through the thatch of his wildly bushy brows. His eyes, half driven into a wrinkly forehead, showed a good deal of white. It looked unsettling and vaguely menacing. Sanpaku Ray.

The two boxes of Georgie's finest sat unopened on the barnboard coffee table. Shpak told us all to sit. Ananah ended up beside me on the couch. Ray slid down the bedroom door into a cross-legged yogi position with hardly any effort. It was amazing, given his bulk. If I tried to do that my knees would pop like champagne corks and my lower legs would fall off. A muffled bark from behind the door confirmed that Gandhi was being kept out of harm's way.

Omar took the chair and clumsily fiddled with the little gun, trying to get the clip back in. It wasn't just that his hands were mangled. I had placed the bullet I'd ejected back in the clip when it was in my pocket, but I put it in the wrong way around. The shell left in the chamber meant it was now just a one-shot gun. After that, the mechanism would be jammed by the backwards shell. Shpak stood by the door sneering at Omar, shaking his head in disbelief.

"You're such a fuckup it's embarrassing."

"What? What?" Omar snivelled in the wearisome lament of the kid who wanted to do right but never could. "I didn't know there was shit in the booze. How could I?"

"I asked you to follow Tough Guy here, to see if he knew anything about the roofies that his bitch of an ex-wife fucking stole. See where he goes, I said. Watch him. Ha!"

"Yeah. Well I did."

"Some surveillance. Where were you hiding, in a tree chipper?"

"It got a little out of control, okay? He suckered me."

I couldn't stifle my grin and it drew Shpak's attention. Fuck him. Since when did his girlfriend suddenly become my ex-wife?

"Your turn is coming, Tough Guy." He turned back to Omar. "When I sent you to get the photos at Janey's what happened?"

"Well fuck, how was I ...?"

Shpak's raised finger silenced him. "You fucked up. That's what happened. And you let this little cunt get hold of them." Pointing to Ananah. "So, I had to go after her but this guy gets in the way." He was pointing at me. Ananah's hand slid over and grabbed my knee in a squeeze of gratitude. Ew.

"Because of that Roman got spooked," he continued, "and now I'm missing not only my partner but some very important papers." This would be Trudy's diaries I thought.

"Yeah, but ..."

"All because of you, you stupid fuck!"

Shpak's rising voice caused Gandhi to start barking.

"Whose fucking dog is barking?"

"The crippled bitch's," said Omar.

"Mine," said Ray.

"Shut it the fuck up," said Shpak.

"Okaay. There, boy. Shh. Noo. Noo," Ray pleaded through the door.

"Now I can't get to my fucking money." Shpak continued his tirade. "Are you listening, asshole?"

"Yeah." Glumly, Omar finally gave up and slid the clip into the butt in what seemed to him to be the wrong way. I watched with a straight face as he painfully cocked the gun the way I had, ejecting the only bullet that would have worked. He made a half-assed grab for the shell but it eluded him and fell to the floor.

"So, I need all that US cash you got. Right now!"

Omar looked hopelessly at me before turning meekly to his big brother.

"You really are a fuckup aren't you, pal," I whispered.

"He's got it." Omar lowered his head and pointed at me.

Shpak's jaw dropped. He looked at Omar like he was something that crawled out of an apple. Then he looked at me, almost with admiration.

"Family!" I said to Shpak and clucked sympathetically, rolling my eyes. He grinned despite himself.

"Best you hand it over then," he told me. Gandhi began to bark again. "Keep that fucking mutt quiet or he's dead," he said to Ray.

"Yass. Okay." Ray was starting to tremble; he tried to shush Gandhi.

"I don't have it on me," I said.

"No?" This time Shpak raised his gun and pointed it at my chest. It was not a comfortable feeling. Nevertheless, I pressed on.

"It's not far. How about I take you to it and you let the rest of these folks go?"

"I got a better idea, Tough Guy." And he reached over and jerked Ananah to her feet. The warmth of her hand, which had been absent-mindedly playing with my leg, went with her.

"Ew. Watch it!" She squealed, trying to hold her torn blouse together while Shpak placed the gun to her head.

"Tell me where the money is now or your little daughter-in-law is dead."

That threw me. I looked at Ray. He looked at me. We both looked at Shpak, then Ananah, and back at each other. I started first, but Ray was right in there: we howled with laughter. Nobody else knew quite what to do. They all wanted to laugh, too, but they didn't get the joke.

As a testament to her doggedness — or lack of sobriety — the front door opened and Dagmar strode into the room. "Jesus fucking Christ," she said, eyeing the scene, setting

Ray and I off even more. Naturally, she thought we were laughing at her. Unfortunately, Gandhi started barking again, providing a focal point for Shpak's frustration. He headed for the bedroom. Ray jumped to his feet and Shpak shot him. Bang. Just like that.

Ray was hit, it looked like in his side, but it didn't stop him or even slow him down. He grabbed Shpak's gun hand and squeezed. You could hear the bones snap. The gun fell to the floor. Next, Ray put his other paw around Shpak's throat, lifted him off his feet and started shaking him like a rag doll. Then he swung him around and threw him against the wall.

Shpak landed upside down, an inert heap. It was not enough. Ray was furious. He walked over, dripping copious amounts of blood, and again picked up his quarry by the neck and shook him viciously. I could only watch. I knew better. Omar, who didn't, crept up and put his little .22 in Ray's ear. Ray swatted him squarely in the chest, a backhand that sent Omar flying past Ananah and over the couch to land at Dagmar's feet as she made to hide in the kitchen. He didn't move after that.

Ray turned his attention back to Shpak. I knew he was calming down a bit because he only swung Shpak around a couple of times before he released the limp rag of a body by heaving it out the open front door. He landed at the feet of Robbie, and three other cops, all of whom had their guns drawn.

Ray staggered to the bedroom, clutching his side. The bullet had gone through him and made a hole in the bedroom door. He opened it frantically and there was doggie doggums, wonderfully intact, wagging his heart-patterned, tail-bereft ass and whimpering as he licked Ray's face like there was no tomorrow.

Robbie stepped into the room tentatively, surveyed the spectacle and slid his gun the rest of the way into his holster. He told the young cop behind him to get an ambulance. Then he saw Omar. "Make that two." I shook my head and pointed to Ray. He saw the blood. "Three, and get them here fast." His eyes scanned the room.

There were dents and heel marks on the wall at eye level where Shpak's feet had grazed them. One of the antique lamps was overturned and sputtering. The venetian blinds had come loose on one side and were hanging in a tilt. The stuffed pheasant was lying on its side on the floor with a broken tail. Ananah stood there in a torn blouse with her brassiereless breasts sticking out. They were in good shape. She was saying, "Omygawd, omygawd," over and over again. Dagmar's mouth was moving, but for once nothing was coming out.

"Ray get mad?" Robbie asked.

"Yep," I said.

"Sorry I missed it," he said and, more thoughtfully, added, "in a way."

Dagmar finally found her voice. "That weird fucking bastard nearly killed Roger," she said to Robbie. "Arrest him."

"How do you know?" asked Robbie.

"Huh?" She blinked. "I saw him. We all fucking saw him."

"No. You said 'nearly.' How do you know he isn't dead all the way?" Robbie gave me a look as we both approached a pale-looking Ray.

"It's starting to hurt a little but I think I'm all right," Ray said to reassure us.

"I hope it hurts a fucking lot!" screamed Dagmar. And there you have it. She was the last to arrive and had the most to say, having no idea about what had gone on before.

Ray spoke up before Robbie or I had a chance. It was a rare moment, because Ray seldom took offence and never gave any. So these were strong words from Ray, as harsh as I have ever heard him speak.

"Smell my ass," he said to Dagmar, just before he fainted.

chapter seventeen

Ananah stood shivering like a kid at the pool, her arms crossed over her chest. She had not moved from where she had been dragged to her feet. The ambulances, now gone, had taken Ray first. Robbie made sure of that. Ray had fought his way back to consciousness to secure our promises to look after Gandhi. Only after he was doubly, triply and quadruply reassured, by me and Robbie, did he agree to be carried by litter bearer to the pasha's golden coach. As befitting his stature, the attendants had wrapped him in a magnificent robe, and carried him in stately procession. Clutched in one hand atop his stomach was a box, the contents cold but still aromatic: provisions for the journey. Ray, Hero of the Realm.

Without thinking much about it I grabbed the velvet matador and tossed him into the corrida once again by draping him around Ananah's shoulders. The furrow of concentration on her brow indicated thought of some complexity. It appeared to be giving her mind quite a workout.

"Thanks, Daddy," she said, coming out of it and wrapping the matador tightly around her. "D'yew think he was really going to, like, shoot me?"

"I don't know. Probably not." Really, I wasn't sure.

"Why did you and the creepy guy laugh so hard when he said it?" She looked at me in a disturbingly direct way. I couldn't hold her gaze.

"The guy might have saved your life, all our lives, so do you think you could drop 'creepy guy' and start calling him Ray?"

"'Kay. Why were you and ... Ray laughing?"

"Nerves, I guess. It was nervous laughter. Besides, it helped throw Shpak off."

"Hmm." She continued to stare at me. Whether it was this, or the fact that we seemed to be having an actual conversation, something was making me very uncomfortable.

Dagmar's voice spread shrilly into the room from the front lawn. She was berating one of the police officers about something. Who bothers to even listen to the whistle and pop of an old radio between stations?

"I have a question for you," I said, as the thought occurred.

"What?" Ananah asked, a little pouty.

"How come you never call her 'Mummy'?"

"Ew, Daddy." She laughed. "As if." And then she slapped me on the arm. It was quite a stinger. Whatever had clouded her thoughts was gone, replaced by the normal blankness in her eyes.

The lesson, learned and forgotten, is to be learned again. Serendipitously it's just in time. I guess if you never had a down day, never missed a shot, never failed to be at peace with yourself, you wouldn't need a lesson: you'd be one. If I had just left matters alone to unfold, as matters do, Ananah would quite likely be dead right now. Instead, with me as an unwitting ally, she lives. Having survived a pair of reasonably concentrated efforts to do her in, she is a walking testament to this. And to the bliss of ignorance.

It was Ananah who wanted the blood tests — not just Donald's, but mine as well. Who knows why? Maybe I blame her for the results. One day you're healthy, if a tad irritable; the next you are no longer someone's father and, oh yeah, dying much sooner than anticipated. Whatever. The lesson I keep needing to learn is acceptance. After that comes understanding. And from now on I will not interfere with anybody else's destiny, no matter how short my stay might be.

We all gave our statements to the police. Once opinion was weaned from fact, Dagmar's, although the lengthiest to collect, proved shortest on paper. I talked to Robbie and told him what had gone down. The money? A fiction contrived by Omar, no doubt to cover his own ass. Robbie didn't believe me, nor did he particularly care. He knew, and I knew, and we left it at that. More importantly he has a little hobby farm just outside the city. Gandhi would stay there until Ray was ready.

The young cop interviewing Ananah seemed very intent on his work. I wondered if this was the guy Shpak conned at the hospital; ending up with his car. To be fair, Robbie said it was not the kid's fault, that his orders were to keep an eye on Shpak, nobody told him outright that it was an arrest.

Every now and again Ananah would make a point by sweeping her arms outward, exposing her breasts. The poor cop's face would turn beet red, and then Ananah would reach out and touch him, creating another visual moment. "Ew, you're, like, sew nice." It was a neat variant of "the flash". The torch had been passed. If I were a betting man, and I am, I'd say that Donald was in for another unpalatable surprise. Maybe because I watched them exchange numbers.

Finally I was left alone with the mess. That is, if you don't count Dagmar and Ananah.

"Why don't you run along home, dear. You're young. You need the rest," Dagmar said.

"And leave Daddy to, like, clean up the mess by himself? I don't think sew." After all, I had saved her life. Twice.

Whether it was the fact that Ananah wouldn't leave, or

that I went to the car to get her one of my T-shirts, I wasn't sure which bothered Dagmar most. That she was upset was enough to add some brightness to the night. And with both of them there each would hold back on whatever their true agenda was.

Ananah knew how to work, at least. She was a thorough cleaner and didn't seem to mind the blood. I worked on the blinds, then taped Weilander's poor pheasant's tail back together after I fixed the lamp. Dagmar sucked candies, smoked, and offered encouragement from the couch. As she finished off the dregs of wine from the cupboard she defended her choice of boyfriends. How could we expect her to know, for fucksakes, and so on.

Then she digressed: "Jesus, you mean there's nothing to drink but this fucking stuff?"

"Not a drop," I said.

"I could make yew some tea." Ananah offered, biting her lip.

"Tea? Tea? Jesus fucking Christ." Then, with the inner divining rod that alcohol lovers seem to have, she fixed her eyes on my discarded jacket. Was it the bulge, or just the way it hung on the back of the wooden chair I had dragged out to fix the blinds? She moved quick as a snake and made a grab for the inside pocket.

"You bastard. What a liar! Nothing to drink, huh? What do you call this?"

Another moral dilemma regarding the unfolding of the universe. Not, apparently, for Ananah, who watched closely but said nothing. I fought the good fight with myself and won. Telling myself not to interfere in this case was sheer sophistry.

"It's poison. Don't drink it."

"Jesus, Frank, since when are you such a goody-goody?"

"No. It's laced with date-rape drug."

"Really? I don't fucking believe you. Why are you keeping it then?"

"It's evidence," I improvised smoothly. "I forgot to give it to Robbie."

"You are such a fucking liar. Why should I believe you?"

"You're right," I said, suddenly getting a swell idea. "I'm such a hog sometimes. Here, hand it over and I'll pour us a drink." She passed the bottle warily, looking at me in an odd way.

"Now I don't trust you. You're up to something, you bastard."

"You think so? I'm going to drink along with you. We'll split it. Unless ... do you want some Scotch, Ananah?"

"Ew. From that? D'yew think I'm stupid?"

She would ask that right at a time when I wasn't one hundred percent sure of the answer. I left her hanging and turned back to Dagmar.

"All the more for us. You take yours neat don't you? So do I."

Without waiting for an answer I went to the kitchen and poured the contents of the bottle into two glasses. I carried them back into the living room and handed one to Dagmar.

"Chin-chin," I said, and took a loud slurpy sip that would have made Ray proud. Wasn't half bad. I took another.

Dagmar just stared at me. She was confused, all the more so because she finally believed the liquor had been doctored. I could see it in her eyes.

"You'd drink that just so I would?" It was a question I didn't need to answer.

"Put the glass down then. You want a drink that bad, go home." My hostility seemed to surprise her. Go figure.

She stood up, blinking back the tears. Humiliated I suppose. I hadn't given her much of an out. She had to leave. That look, the old black and white photograph where the three-year-old is shading her eyes, looking off into the distance for mummy, is on her face.

The telephone rang. It was six in the morning, eight Toronto time, which is where Lynnmarie was calling from. Such a beautiful voice. Like music.

"I know it's early, but I have to talk to you." She said.

"You can call anytime you want. What's up?" I asked, walking into the kitchen for privacy.

"I tried to reach you before you left."

"Oh yeah? I thought we weren't on good terms."

"I was angry, okay? Don't make me feel worse."

"Did I tell you how great it is to hear your voice?"

"Do you mean that?"

"Yeah."

"Maybe you'll feel differently in a minute."

"Never."

The front door made quite a racket as it slammed. I peeked around the corner and saw Ananah, tiny yellow feathers dropping from her mouth. Dagmar was gone.

"What was that?" asked Lynnmarie, more than a little frostily.

"Another graceful exit by mummy dearest."

"She was there with you?" The frost turned into a deep freeze.

"Easy," I laughed. "When you phoned I was in a little rubber dinghy eating cold pizza and watching two pink, triangular dorsal fins circle. Now there's only one."

"Someone is still there?"

"Yep."

"Not the daughter-in-law?"

"The very same."

"Good god!"

"So give me a break. Fuck, what a night. I can't wait to tell you."

"If you're still talking to me."

"Why would you say that?"

"I've done something a little stupid," she said, after a long pause. Now there's a phrase calculated to send your balls hiking back up into your pelvic cavity.

"Jesus, Babe, I don't know if I want to hear this right now. Do I want to hear this?"

"Idiot! It's about your blood test."

"Oh, you know about that? Sorry." I was relieved, until

I thought about the test. "I didn't want you to think I was trying for sympathy."

"Of course I know. After all, I work here."

"Here? Isn't it kind of early for you to be at the clinic?"

"Yes, but that's the point. I had to correct something, and you're a big part of it."

"I have an idea. Instead of being so direct why don't you just talk in circles and I'll try to guess what it is."

"Sorry. It's just that you're going to hate me." This time I didn't say anything, forcing her to get on with it. Finally in a rush she said, "I switched the results of your blood test."

Once again surf was up, and pounding in my ears. What was I hearing?

"Frank?"

"Yeah."

"Did you hear me? I switched the results. I'm so sorry."

"You wanted me to think I was dying?"

"No. Oh god. That was a total accident. I only found out yesterday."

"I'm not dying?"

"It was the paternity issue. I was so sick of the way Donald was treating you, and with you putting up with it, making excuses for him. Dagmar too. The cow. So I switched tests, unfortunately with someone who ..."

"So I'm not dying."

"No. Now you hate me, right?"

"If you only knew how good it is to talk to you right now."

"Really?"

"Really." And it was.

"So did you start smoking again?"

"Not yet."

"I thought you would."

"I could never get past the menthol."

"What do you mean?"

"Long story. Tell you when I get back."

"This must have been so hard for you. I'm really sorry. It was a stupid thing to do."

"Nah. It was a trip. You know, stay centred, let it all go, and bam: you're there." I don't think I'll ever tell her how close the timing was, how close Donald came to being an orphan. It would probably have been good for him.

"Where do you want me to send your actual results?"

"Throw them away."

"Are you sure?"

"For now, at least."

"What about the wedding?"

"I seriously doubt it will ever happen. Not anytime soon, for sure. I'll tell you all about it when I see you." Most of it anyway.

"No wedding, after all the shit they put you through?"

"Yup."

"Those jerks. Well, have you had enough yet?"

"As a matter of fact, yes. Know what, though?"

"What?"

"When I get over feeling good I'm going to be really pissed off at you."

"Not that pissed," she said softly.

"You don't think so?"

"No. I don't."

She had me there.

After the call I poured the two glasses into the sink. I was drowsy but couldn't tell how much was due to relief. Ananah was making some sort of case on her own behalf, saying that Donald had depleted her financial resources. It was a negotiation that was interrupted by the black fog that suddenly descended upon me. It would have done no good to fight it, so I succumbed.

I made the circuitous, groggy journey back to consciousness in darkness. I lay on my back between the sheets. "Where am I?" became the question, but the answer proved elusive. Pieces of dreams floated in and out. I think Trudy was in one of the more delicious ones. Except she was smaller, more lithe. Definitely a younger Trudy; more giving, with blonder hair and bangs. I tried to sit up but couldn't. Some time in the night I had to pee and needed to be helped to my feet. I was guided to the bathroom, where I had to sit to do my business. Then I was lifted to my feet again. That was the beginning of the Trudy dream, I think. Someone led me back to bed by grabbing my ever stiffening penis and guiding it like a tiller. "Again?" she was saying. "Well, if you insist."

My entire body ached but nothing more than my stomach. The muscles were shot with the strain of combat. I had to inch my way to the side of the bed and kick my feet over the edge to get enough momentum to sit up. Fighting is definitely a young man's sport. It took forever to dress, every move an agony. It would be better once I started moving around. The clock on Weilander's night table said eight. So did my watch. Over thirteen hours of sleep and I was still tired.

It was too late to visit Ray, so I phoned Robbie. The station told me he was at home. They gave me his number when I identified myself. His wife answered: we go way back.

"Yes, Ray is fine and so is the dog," she said in answer to my question. "I'm fine, too; thanks for asking. But how are you, Frank? I hear you had an interesting evening."

"I'm in great shape, Mandy, as long as I don't have to move."

She laughed then clucked a little and handed me to Robbie. We talked a while. Ray was coming along splendidly, but he was so heavily sedated that a visit could wait until tomorrow. I hardly even listened to the rest. Robbie was feeling pretty damned good about putting Shpak and Omar away, though. I was suddenly lonesome and just wanted to get on a plane and go home. I spotted the note after I had hung up.

"Thanks daddy." It said. "I guess I cant call you that anymore but its kind of like a habit. You saved my life. I wont forget. Dont forget to send the money. I wont tell anybody about you know what unless you forget the money. Ha ha just a joke. To bad about the wedding. We just arnt ready yet." It was signed with the outline of a heart with the letter 'A' in the middle. "P.S. You can send the two thousand to this address. Soon is good. A."

I vaguely remember agreeing to give her money before I crashed out. Two thousand sounds about right. And I knew the wedding was going to be called off. As to whatever else she was talking about, I'm drawing a complete blank. Oh well. Ananah was no different than a bird, really. Survival requires that you seek every advantage possible. And she was some survivor.

chapter eighteen

Weilander met me at the airport three weeks to the day from when I had gone back to Toronto. He was just finishing a survey for the university when he had run across several large, tame flocks of sharptail grouse and Hungarian partridge down around the US border near Rockglen. By then I had worked up quite a yearning to go out at least one more time. Lynnmarie was not pleased, but since I had recently faced my imminent demise, I was seeing some things differently — and braver than I ought to be. She only has herself to blame for that. Besides, despite the fact I couldn't get back to her fast enough, things were a bit flat between us. Who knows where that will lead?

It was the countryside around Rockglen and the drive to get there that attracted me as much as the hunting. Situated between the badlands to the east and Grasslands National Park to the west, it's like the last of the real Wild West; the west of buttes, sagebrush and rolling hills; country that makes you want to use words and phrases like "s'posin'", "'pears like" and "I reckon" as you pass through. Yippie ki-yi-ay and all that.

We were going to open the season together. Weilander was driving a brand new half-ton. "Courtesy of the biology department, eh. It's a rental and all mine for another week. Jeez, this is going to be great. The place is crawling with chickens and huns."

"I brought you something," I said, when we got back to his place. I handed him a shoebox wrapped elegantly with old newspaper. It was a junk mail sculpture I had worked on for two days.

"Oh yeah? This would be one of your stupid things, I guess."

He tore open the wrapper to reveal the close approximation of canine testicles I had fashioned out of leather and two large marbles. I had fixed them to a wooden trophy store plaque. "Nemesis No More" was engraved on a little copper tag underneath.

"I want to show you something you might find interesting," he said, with the air of a man who was suitably pleased with himself, and led me to the basement.

He flicked a switch and a small spotlight illuminated something covered with a dropcloth on his workbench. The unveiling revealed that Weilander had definitely got the better of me. It was his hound from hell, his devil dog, stuffed and mounted, still looking eerie and menacing. One rear leg was raised in a familiar, disdainful pose. Closer inspection showed that my plaque had not done justice to the beast. They don't make marbles big enough.

"It's magnificent, Weilander, absolutely magnificent!" He obviously thought so too.

"It's for a diorama at the museum, eh. Twentieth-century urban fauna. I did this guy first," he said, patting it condescendingly on the rump.

"So how did you get him, Slick, or was it that big tire iron in the sky?"

"Well," he said, looking suddenly concerned. "I have to talk to you about that. Coupla things, actually. But it has to stay between you and me, eh. No matter what. It's confidential. And it's not about Dagmar, if that's what you're thinking. Jeez, she's not even talking to me. What did I do? Anyway, it goes no further than here. Agreed?"

He was wanting to tell me so badly that I negotiated a few caveats before I consented to total confidentiality.

"First, I was right about the gun. You know, when someone shot at you and Ray. It was a .243 Remington pump, but she was just trying to scare you. She felt bad about the dog, eh. Didn't even see him."

"She? Who are you talking about?"

"Glennie."

"Glennie? Jesus, Weilander, what the fuck is going on? Trying to scare me? Why?"

"She saw you outside the bar that night with Ananah. Said she waved at you and you ignored her. She got mad, eh. A few too many. She was bringing my gun into town, so she followed you. When you and Ray came out she got the bright idea to take a couple of pot shots. Jeez, I'm sorry, man. She is, too, 'specially since she found out it was only your daughter-in-law."

"She's fucking crazy. I always thought Lenore was the weird one."

"And speaking of Lenore ..." Weilander said.

"Oh no. There's more?"

"There might be." He shot me a kind of helpless look, peculiar to him in emotional situations. Sort of like a basset; mournful, seeking solace. I had to laugh.

"See, Robbie came to see me at Lenore's the next day, after Ray cleaned Shpak's clock. Fuck, did you know he was that strong? Jeez. So Robbie parks out front and Lenore says, 'O, lordy, they're back.' Who's back? I ask. 'The cops,' she says. That's just Robbie, I say. Then I ask her who else was here? 'Just some cop,' she says. 'A big one. He was here yesterday nosing around.' So I knew it was Fat Boy, eh, looking for me. Then she said, 'I hid in the garage. He looked in there and then he stole one of my sausages.' Sausages? I say, because Lenore is almost a vegetarian. 'Yeah,' she says. 'One of the kielbossas I was fixing up.' Fixing up? Whaddya mean fixing up? I ask. But she clammed up. Wouldn't say anything else.

"Anyway, a couple days later, Lenore drives over and says, 'I got something for you in the trunk.' What? I say. 'Come and see,' she says. So I unwrap a green garbage bag and there's Fido from hell. 'He won't bother you any more,' she says. I knew for sure then. It wasn't just what Robbie said about Fat Boy choking, and the poison in the meat. I mean, I got a thing about dogs but Lenore, well, she's another story. So I say, Lenore, you gotta stop killing all these dogs. And she says, 'I know, I know,' and starts blubbering. 'This is the last one, honest,' she says. Well, fuck. I mean, I don't know what to do. Whaddya think?"

"Well, I'd sure be avoiding family dinners if I were you."

"Fuuck. No kidding. Really though, ya think I should do something?"

"Is she stopped?"

"I think so. I hope so."

"Wait and see then before you do anything."

"That's what I'm thinking."

"There is one thing, though."

"What?"

"Don't ever tell Ray."

"Jeez, you can bet your ass on that. I hear Shpak's still in traction. Hey, how's Ray doing?"

"He's still in the hospital, but he should be out soon. He sounds pretty much the same as usual."

It was a concern, Ray not being released. Usually hospitals have you walking out the door as soon as you can move one leg. Besides, they're such depressing environments that you're happy to oblige. But every time I had talked to Ray on the phone he seemed quite chipper. My afternoon visit provided some illumination.

It was lunchtime, or just after, judging by the trays being wheeled around. As I approached Ray's room I spotted an old Asian guy with a huge grin nodding and looking in the direction from whence Ray's falsetto trilled.

"Were you going to eat that, Mr. Chow?"

"No. Take it. You eat," the old boy said. "Look good when

you eat. Sound good too. Ha ha."

I walked in as Ray stole across the room and grabbed a pudding cup from Mr. Chow's tray. He was wearing the airy regulation hospital gown with the slit up the back. The only thing hairier than Ray's chest, arms and face was his ass, legs and back. From behind, he looked like an overfed bear that had escaped from a barber shop. The debris around Ray's tray showed evidence of similar expeditions to the other two occupants of the room, both of whom were snoring the afternoon away, their wispy white hair sticking up from under the covers.

"I guess I shouldn't have brought this, then," I said, wielding the extra large concoction I had picked up at Georgie's.

"Frank! It's so good to see you." Ray's eyes were firmly fixed on the pizza box.

"You look pretty healthy to me, Ray."

"Mmmm. I thought I smelled something grand," he replied, just as a muffled retort sounded from under one of his roommate's blankets. "But then you never can be sure," he added, rolling his eyes.

"So you want it then, or is it too soon after lunch?"

"Your timing couldn't be better. I could really use a palate cleanser." He opened the box and gazed upon the contents in awe, like an urchin with a new bike.

Remembering his manners, just barely, he introduced me to Mr. Chow and asked would either of us care to partake. We declined and Ray set about demolishing his gustatory windfall.

"Good eater," declared Mr. Chow.

"The best," I agreed.

"Yes, number one for sure," the old man beamed, glowing with genuine pleasure.

During my visit, at roughly five-minute intervals, some member of the hospital staff — an orderly, nurse, doctor, or whoever — would happen by. "How are you today, Ray?" "Can I get you anything, Ray?" "Let me fix that pillow for you." And so on. Ray was flourishing with the attention.

"So how long have you been well enough to be released, Raymond?"

"Just over a week," he said. "Goodness, there are so many nice people here it's going to be hard to leave. But tomorrow is the day,"

Ray showed me a beautiful hand-painted card from Gandhi, signed with a paw print.

"There's a basement suite in Joe's house where Gandhi and I shall be quite welcome," Ray said, reminding me that I had two envelopes, one for him and one for Joe.

"What's this for?" he asked.

"It's for nothing."

"In that case I accept. Thank you." And he gave a little bow.

Ray asked about Donald. I told him that Ananah had called the wedding off, saying they needed more time. A hundred years ought to do it.

"Lucky for her," he said.

"No. I'm finished with that business, Ray. Let what will be, be.

I also told him about Donald's message, left on my machine, accusing me of destroying his life and ruining his fucking marriage. So I won't be looking him up just yet. Perhaps it won't be a hundred years. I did send him saying number forty-nine from Lao Tzu. The Bynner translation, of course.

It goes like this:

> A sound man's heart is not shut within itself
> But is open to other people's hearts:
> I find good people good,
> And I find bad people good
> If I am good enough;
> I trust men of their word
> And I trust liars
> If I am true enough;

I feel the heart beat of others
Above my own
If I am enough of a father,
Enough of a son.

Maybe some day Donald will discover this father-son business is a two-way street.

"So, if I don't see you after hunting, Ray, I'll be back for the trial."

"Oh that."

"Yeah that. And I heard Trudy was going to be the judge," I said, having heard no such thing.

"Really?" he said, somewhat smugly. "Well then, I might just hang on to her diaries a while longer."

"You have them?" I asked, astonished.

"Wouldn't you like to know."